Three Men on a

Pilgrimage

A Comical Progress

Thomas Jones

WHISPERING TREE

Whispering Tree Original Books
http://www.whisperingtreeoriginalbooks.com

ISBN: 978-0-9927363-2-3

Printed in the United Kingdom
Book Design: M² Media Marek Mularczyk - Soul Travel Lodge

Contents

Chapter 1   1

I discover the existence of sin. We determine to redeem ourselves.

Chapter 2   7

The necessary existence of suffering.

Chapter 3   17

Disbelief, stemming from ignorance of the beliefs rejected.

Chapter 4   24

How religion has been used in the past for purposes for which it was never intended.

Chapter 5   31

Evolution and religion. How Christianity is unnatural, and therefore good.

Chapter 6   38

On Christian perfection.

Chapter 7   43

How each religion sees part of the elephant, or would do if it weren't for Health & Safety.

Chapter 8   **48**

How people, having rejected traditional religions, find a gap in their lives, and how they find substitutes that are not replacements.

Chapter 9   **54**

If so many people have all experienced God, surely there must be something there to experience, even if the description isn't always the same.

Chapter 10   **60**

How morality is multi-layered and not at all straight forward. How Christians are expected to do better.

Chapter 11   **68**

The case against the biblical view of homosexuality and the doctrine of Hell.

Chapter 12   **76**

The pure reason for doing good is that we have already been rewarded in full. Or on how Christianity is all back to front.

Chapter 13   **81**

The nature of Christ. How unlikely is something that has happened, and will only happen, once?

Chapter 14   **85**

On the existence of moral atheists. Why they can exist, but could do better.

Chapter 15   **90**

Denying something because you've never

experienced it yourself is small-mindedness of the worst kind.

Chapter 16   96

How religions cannot be held responsible for those that do not follow their commandments, even if they claim to be adherents.

Chapter 17   102

On the concept of the Trinity.

Chapter 18   107

On an Interventionist God and the nature of miracles.

Chapter 19   111

Speculations on the Afterlife, and the nature of body and soul.

Chapter 20   114

On denominations and the purpose of the Holy Spirit.

Chapter 21   120

The foolishness of blaming God for failing to answer prayers.

Chapter 22   125

On the nature of evil.

Chapter 23   133

On blaming God for the existence of suffering.

Chapter 24   138

On doing as we would be done by.

Chapter 25   143

Of our inability to save ourselves, but the ability to accept or deny salvation, and do so more than once.

Chapter 26   148

On the diminishing need for God in a world of science.

Chapter 27   155

On how science may not have removed the need for God, but may have removed the need for a Devil.

Chapter 28   161

On faith and works.

Chapter 29   165

On the belief in the divinity, or otherwise, of Christ.

Chapter 30   174

On the idea that religion is merely a prop for the morally and intellectually weak.

Chapter 31   179

The 'invention' of God.

Chapter 32   186

The universe according to atheists.

Chapter 33   194

On Free Will and the merits of choice as opposed to forced compliance.

Chapter 34   **201**

On the irrationality of the universe.

Chapter 35   **204**

On the trappings of long-established denominations.

Chapter 36   **211**

On the dual nature of Christ.

Chapter 37   **215**

That you can only disregard certain of and so many elements of Christianity before what you have left isn't worth having.

Chapter 38   **223**

Why some level of organised religion is still important.

Chapter 39   **227**

Our destination? Thoughts on continual grace.

Chapter 40   **232**

We arrive. Financial difficulties and an unexpected obstacle.

Chapter 41   **241**

Salvation. The journey home. Our pilgrimage begins.

Acknowledgements   **248**

About the Author   **249**

For Caroline, always

Chapter 1

I discover the existence of sin. We determine to redeem ourselves.

The three of us were sitting in my living room talking about how bad we were, in a moral and spiritual sense, that is.

"You know," G. began, "I think I must be the most miserable, hell-bound sinner you could ever hope to meet."

"No, no, no!" B. replied. "I can hardly believe that you're quite as wicked as me. I'm so firmly set on the wide and sloping path that there can surely be no one quite as bad as myself."

I simply shook my head at my friends' presumptions. In reality, they were both more-or-less decent chaps and these delusions of depravity were simply attention-seeking of the worst kind. If the citizens of the diabolic world below were half as bad as my poor self, there simply wouldn't be room for mere dabblers-in-sin such as my two companions.

§

It all started with a pair of those well-meaning fellows who gamely go round knocking on doors. Now, I can't help but feel that these people possibly do more harm than good to the perception of Christianity in the great soup of general ignorance that we call the popular mentality, but you must admit that they're not easily discouraged. In the face of such regular rejection, scorn and downright abuse, they soldier on where the rest of us would surely have thrown in the towel and decided that the horrible people at number seventy-four could stew in the juice of their own tragic atheism for all we cared.

So it was that two of these smartly suited fellows came round to my house and started talking at me. Once I could get a word in slantwise, I explained that I wasn't much interested and would be grateful if they could go away please, if they didn't mind too much. I was as polite and friendly as possible; they took the hint and we parted on good terms. However, they left a small leaflet in my hands as a sort of parting shot. I put it on the coffee table in the living room and quite forgot about it.

Some hours later, I was having a cup of tea and happened to notice it. In a moment of unthinking weakness, I picked it up and started to flick through it. It turned out to be a rather anxious leaflet on the subject of 'The Sins' and sin in general. I read all about avarice, and was suddenly struck by the shocking realisation that I had well and truly got it! Next came gluttony and, on reading of it, I became convinced that I had that too, just as I was reaching for a third custard cream. Then I became interested in my own case and decided to sift myself from top to bottom.

Avarice I had in a most severe form, in which I couldn't see something I lacked without becoming convinced that it was the only thing in the entire universe that would make life bearable for even a second longer. I believe I can trace it back to when I was very small and saw an enormous toy castle in a shop. Being young and not owning an awful lot at that size, it struck me that if there was a single thing in the entire world that I must possess, above all food, drink or other sustenance, above air, earth and sky, it was that specific, single castle. Fortunately for my miniature self, my parents were wise and recognised the early signs of a severe and lifelong form of avarice. They did not buy that castle. I have never forgiven them and still bring it up at Christmas in the hope that they will see the error of their ways and finally get it for me.

Lust, I'd had since the age of thirteen or so, and have been a martyr to it ever since, at every opportunity. I felt it had peaked a little in my late teens and was now abating slightly. Nonetheless, it afflicts me terribly every time a pretty young woman walks by.

Gluttony came and went with the ebb and flow of my finances (if only I had more money... avarice again!), but, when I could, I did and did as much as I could. Satisfaction to me means a full belly and a full glass. Full of what, I am not too particular about. If I do suffer from gluttony, at least in my case it is not a petty, narrow-minded sort of sin. It is wide, accepting and all-consuming.

Jealousy, I've had as much as the next fellow. I think that perhaps it's faded a little with age, but that might just be me getting used to the symptoms. Certainly I don't get green-eyed over women or such things, but when I was younger, I was fit to burst when I went round a certain friend's house and viewed his comprehensive and utterly unfair collection of action figures and associated play-sets, Ghostbusters cars and so forth. Also, my neighbours don't own a donkey, so I'm safe in that department.

Wrath. I'm not too sure about this. If I don't get sufficient hours' sleep a night and I'm starved of food for more than five or six hours, I most definitely get rather snappish. A trifle irritable, y'know? But who wouldn't? I'm sure that all the saints must have been grumpy if deprived of sleep. We are informed (that is, I'm sure I remember reading somewhere once) that the Duke of Wellington (not a saint, but extremely historical) wasn't at his best unless he got twelve hours' sleep a day, and I think I must be cast in the same mould, which means, of course, that I oscillate between mild wrath and moderate sloth. If I stay in bed long enough to stave off Vesuvian rage, I find myself guilty of laziness. If I get up bright and early, the first chap who wishes me a "Good morning!" gets a solid right-hook to the jaw.

In fact, reading through this leaflet, the only sin I could conclude I didn't really have was pride. At first, I was crestfallen. It seemed only right, for the sake of completeness if nothing else, that I be a proud fellow, as well as angry, lazy, lustful, jealous and all the rest. But upon consideration, I realised that it was probably a good thing. I was a sinner, it was true, but at least I didn't brag about it. I was a humble sinner. Indeed, if you can credit it, I was a good sinner. A sinner, but better than most, if not as good as many. And this realisation made me angry. Why couldn't other people do as well as me? I wasn't really trying, I had fallen at every other hurdle, but at least I'd gotten over the last one, and that without any effort at all. Surely other, wiser people than me could do just as well? Could I be the only humble sinner? Surely not, and yet I had not met any others. G. and B. were prideful rogues at the best of times, without inflating their egos any further with talk of hurdles.

This last small but significant victory aside, I seemed to have failed at every turn. I opened that leaflet a happy, satisfied and fulfilled chap. I put it down a miserable and penitent sinner.

❧

"What we need," G. said, "is a holiday to take our minds off it. No use worrying about it, my mother used to say. We're bound for the sulphur and brimstone, so we might as well have as much fun out of the terrestrial existence as possible. Am I right?"

"Well..." said B., "if there is nothing we can do..." He looked at me hopefully. After all, it was I who had read the leaflet and so, as far as they were concerned, I was a Theologian. Practically reverend, if not quite right.

I took my new-found responsibilities seriously and considered the question carefully.

"It seems to me, that there is quite a lot we could do. It seems to me that what we need isn't just a holiday, what we need is to go and getting some jolly good spiritualling before the end. A bit of the old repent and recant sort of thing."

G. looked doubtful. "I'm not sure that ashes and sack cloth are in this year. Not the thing to wear to the races in any case. More high street you might say." A vain man, G. One of his other failings.

"No," I replied. "I wasn't thinking of flagellant penitenting or anything like that. How about a pilgrimage?"

"A pilgrimage?" B. looked aghast. "Where on earth to?"

"Canterbury seems popular for those sorts of things. Chaucer and the like."

"That's true. Very literary."

"And," G. put in cheerfully, "it's not all that far away. A couple of tents, some sleeping bags and so on. It'll be a pleasant walking holiday. Only religious. Good for body, mind and soul and that sort of thing."

It was decided. The three of us (oh, and Montgomery, G.'s dog, who added a Blytonian aspect to the proceedings) were going on a pilgrimage to Canterbury, for the good of our souls and, as B. pointed out, the detriment of our wallets. Preparations were set in motion.

Chapter 2

The necessary existence of suffering.

We made the necessary arrangements regarding time off work for good behaviour and so forth, decided on dates, figured out what we wanted to take with us and even glanced at a map. Fortunately, it was the height of summer when we decided that we needed a little religious experience under our belts, so it actually sounded like an all-round pleasant sort of jaunt, religion or no, and this got me wondering.

"I say, fellas?" I began hesitantly.

B. looked up from the tent he was trying to re-pack. He had unpacked it to make sure everything was there, all the time complaining about what a devil it was to pack up. Now some of the language he was using was making me think this whole endeavour was doomed from the start.

"Yes?"

"I've been thinking…"

"Oh no!"

"Ahem! I've been thinking; does it really count if it's going to be a holiday?"

G. looked up from his road map. "Pardon?"

"Well, it seems to me that a pilgrimage should be a solemn sort of affair, with spiritual contemplation going hand in hand with physical hardship and deprivation, possibly interspersed with the telling of comic tales on horseback."

"Well, back in the day, I suppose so. But this is the modern age. We don't have deprivations nowadays."

"Or horses!" piped in B. "Well, not so many anymore. And they're not really used for comic tales. Oh, except this one I heard from my cousin. I say, this horse walks into a pub..."

"Well, it seems like we shouldn't be... well... enjoying it as such."

"You think we should be trading in the macs and thermoses for sackcloth and ashes? A couple of scourges and so on?"

"...and he goes up to the bar you see, this horse..."

"No, of course not. I mean... dash it, I don't know! It just seems like we should be enjoying it for what it is, not thinking of it as a walking holiday with a purpose."

"... and the barman, the barman he... ha ha ha!... he says, to this horse, he says..."

"I see what you mean. Maybe we should keep the aim in mind, and if we happen to enjoy ourselves along the way, just accept it as a sort of bonus."

I nodded. "That seems reasonable. But no frivolous enjoyment, understand?"

"Perfectly."

"... why the long face?"

"Pardon?"

"Oh, um... nothing."

ᦕ

So, on a sunny summer's morn, we set forth on our quest for fresh air, exercise and a little spiritual enlightenment.

B. was thinking as he walked. I could tell. There was a sort of low hum in the air, and I could smell burning metal. I knew what had caused it; I could indicate with pin-point accuracy what had set off this bout of mental exertion.

We had been ready to set off, bags packed, tents lurking within, sleeping bags rolled and ready, food prepped, thermoses filled and every other thing ship-shape and Bristol fashion. All we had to do was put on our walking boots. Mine were new, as were G's. B., however, had old boots. 'Worn in' he called them. 'Done in' G. had replied. Poor Montgomery had taken one sniff and rolled on his back, feet in the air in the time-honoured fashion of dead animals since feet had been invented.

Anyhow, B.'s boots, such as they were, were crusted with the mud and gunge of a hundred short walks under inclement conditions. He had sagely put them in a plastic bag so as to save G.'s carpet and his own skin. He brought them out onto the doorstep to put on and, in doing so, stubbed his toe most savagely on the boot-scraper. As soon as the echoes of his agonised squeals had faded into nothingness, and the neighbour's cat had been coaxed back down from the roof, trembling and cross-eyed, his brain rumbled into motion.

Now, some three quarters of an hour later, he was ready to make some epoch-shattering pronouncement of infinite sagacity and insight. He opened his mouth, breathed in, and spoke thus:

"God," he said, "is a bit of a rum cove really. A bit unpleasant."

I nodded, wondering how best to receive this gem. I decided that I needed further clarification.

9

"In what sense old fellow? I've always heard people speak quite highly of him. I'm not sure he'd sue you for defamation, but nonetheless it seems a little incautious."

"This morning, I stubbed my toe."

"You did as well!" G. chipped in. "I remember it distinctly. I've never seen a man shatter earthenware with a shriek before."

"It was not a shriek! It was a... sharp exclamation."

"I'll say. I could have used that exclamation to chop firewood, then shave with it when I'd done."

"Anyway, it seems distinctly unfair that I should stub my toe while preparing to set off on a pilgrimage. He should be happy for me, smoothing my path and easing my hardships. But does he? No! He puts a beastly sharp boot-scraper right where my toe was about to be. He introduced pain into my life in no small way."

"I think we're drifting into deep waters here," I cautioned. "Even greater minds than ours must have considered why God would inflict boot-scrapers on a penitent toe."

"I think it's just beastliness. If He really wanted us to succeed, He would have removed all boot-scrapers, right from the beginning. He could have proclaimed on the eighth day, once He was feeling Himself again, 'Let There Be No Boot-scrapers'. It would have been easy for Him, but no. In His idleness, He allowed boot-scrapers into the world, to harry the sons of men."

I gave this some serious consideration. "Well, I suppose He wouldn't want to make it too easy, would He?"

"Why on earth not? Why wouldn't he make it easy to come to Him? He'd get far more people if it was easy. If He makes it hard, He's just losing a huge amount of his intended demographic. Instead, He fills life with things that actively bar the way. He fills the world with fear, despair and wrought-iron boot-scrapers!"

"But if there were no boot-scrapers," G. pointed out, "how would you get the mud off your boots?"

"I would use a brush."

"But you'd have to take off your boots to go inside and get the brush."

"So?"

"And therefore you'd probably go and stub your toe on the doorstep, and now you'd be complaining because there *wasn't* a boot-scraper."

"Quite right." I agreed. "It seems to me that in this world of ours, most things are created for, or at least capable of being, used by us. However, the nature of the world means that anything that is used can equally be misused, accidentally or otherwise."

"But I didn't misuse it." B. complained. "It sat there and allowed me to stub my toe on it."

"But there may well be parallel universes," I replied, "in which somewhere, a B. is getting told off by a G. for scraping his horrible muddy boots all over G.'s nice shiny toe-stubber."

"It's just the thing he'd do," G. agreed. "Messing up other people's toe-stubbers."

"I would not!"

"And then you'd be complaining that if a toe-stubber wasn't meant to be used for cleaning boots, why would it be made in such a shape that you could scrape your boots on it."

He didn't have an answer to this. Deep, inky waters indeed. I was just rallying myself for another stab at it all when I was mercifully saved by a sudden wailing shriek. It came with such suddenness and volume that the three of us near leapt out of our skins and into the river. We were by this point walking along an extremely pleasant path running along a riverbank, weeping willows dipping melancholy boughs into the soothing waters, and kingfishers swooping on glittering wing as though they owned the place. Tranquil I would have called it, but for the screaming.

Well, it was obvious that murder most foul was being done to some poor body in the close vicinity, and it goaded us into action. We would not be found wanting when innocent life and limb were in danger. Looking at each other, stunned for a second, we broke into a run (well, in B.'s case a slightly accelerated amble), heading for the source of the ruckus.

The screaming and wailing only got louder, and I couldn't help but wonder if we would save the poor devil only for them to be fined by the Waterways people for noise pollution. Such is the age in which we live!

We turned a corner in the path and found ourselves at the scene of the crime. And what a crime! A vile, cowardly devil with the brutish look of the born killer was holding a small child under the water. The child was struggling to keep its head above the surface, and was the one producing such an impressively voluble cry.

The man looked up as we came charging round the corner with some surprise, and stopped trying to drown the poor kid, holding him up, no doubt, in an attempt to look innocent. I now had a moment to fully take in the details of the scene in order to fully describe them to the police, and couldn't help but admire the planning and thought that had gone into the thing. No sudden crime of passion this! Why, the chap had even thought to bring a swimming costume with him so as not to ruin his day clothes, which would no doubt be re-donned to make his escape. Quite why he'd bothered dressing the little fellow in swimming trunks was beyond me though. This is why we employ police inspectors. They understand the workings of the criminal mind you see, not like us fortunate everyday fellows who'd rather not plumb the depths.

I suddenly realised that we had unwittingly made ourselves targets for this crazed child-killer's next massacre. Remove all the witnesses and so forth. Before he could spring at us though, I turned to B.

"Run! Find a policeman!" I cried. "We'll hold him off!" B. turned and shambled as fast as possible along the path and out of sight. I turned back to the maniac, who was staring at us open-mouthed. Overcome, no doubt, by the realisation that the game was up.

"Aha!" I said.

The savage looked at me politely. Not the reaction I'd expected, so I thought I'd try it again.

"Aha!"

"Good afternoon. I'm sorry about the noise, but you know how it is."

I blinked. I glanced at G., who looked equally stunned. Not the sort of thing you expect nor want to hear from a vile murderer of children. Not the kind of person whom you'd like to think of as talking to you on a professional level.

"Well, no, not really."

"Oh? You don't have children then?"

"Um, not yet, no."

"Ah. Well you can imagine I'm sure. Just one of those things you have to do once they reach a certain age. They'd only have to go through it later in school, and it's such an advantage for them to get it over and done with now."

"I… um… yes, well of course I maybe went to a different sort of school but… uh…"

"And the river is so much more private than a public swimming pool. Warmer too!" He gave a little laugh.

I floundered. I could definitely feel the situation sliding out of my grasp, and G. was standing with his mouth open like the Channel Tunnel. I decided to start again.

"Aha!"

"Yes?"

"Let the child go base villain!"

"Pardon?"

I hesitated. "Um, the child. Let him go." I paused. "Um... base... villain."

He looked at the child in his arms, then up at me. The boy had stopped struggling and was staring up at me in that solemn way small children have. Strange creatures really.

"Why?" the fellow asked.

"What do you mean, 'why'?"

"Why do you want me to put my son down?"

"Because otherwise he'll drown. Foul criminal!"

"But if I put him down, he will drown!"

"Not straight down! I mean let him go! Return him to the safety of the river bank. Brutal fiend!"

He was about to reply when B. came puffing and panting round the corner with an equally breathless bobby in tow.

"Officer!" I cried. "Arrest that man!"

The chap in the water jumped. "What? Why?"

"Because," I paused dramatically, "he is trying to murder that child!"

The perfidious ne'er-do-well stood dumbstruck for several seconds. "I'm what?"

"Aha!" G. cried, eager to get in on the accusations. "Don't try and deny it. We heard the child screaming. You were caught in the act of trying to drown him!"

"Drown him? No! I love my son, why wou…"

"Lying wretch!" I interrupted. G. had broken my flow and rather stolen my thunder, and I wanted it back. "The child was suffering. You were holding him scant seconds and inches from a watery death when we found you."

"Well, yes, I suppose that's true in a manner of speaking but…"

"You see!" B. shouted, having finally gotten his breath back and equally eager for the limelight. "He admits it."

"Now listen!" the fellow yelled. "And no interrupting either! Now," he continued more calmly, "yes, it's true that I was technically holding my son in peril. He was cold and afraid, and in danger of death. But," he said loudly as I tried to speak, "my child knows that I love him and want the best for him. He knows that if he trusts me and lets me hold him, even if it seems like I'm being unnecessarily cruel, if he doesn't try and break free, and allows me to support him, no matter how close to danger, and believes that I will never let him go, eventually, he will learn to swim."

ꙮ

As we walked away, having apologised both to the fellow and to the policeman, I turned to B. and G.

"You know, I'm sure that there is a lesson in here somewhere, but I'll be blown if I can figure out what it is."

"I say!" said B. "Look at that."

I followed his pointing finger. The river bank sloped gently down to the water here, giving rise to a long, narrow sort of sandy beach. "What?"

"Well you see those footprints?"

"Yes? Could it perhaps mean that we're not the first to

walk along this river bank?"

"But there're two sets of footprints for most of the way, except for the really gravely, stony bits. Then there's only one set."

"So? Maybe they walked on the grass. That's what I'd do."

"Or," G. pointed out, "maybe one of them was drunk and kept falling in."

"Oh. Yes. Good point."

We continued along the river.

Chapter 3

Disbelief, stemming from ignorance of the beliefs rejected.

The next day, after a more-or-less passable night in our tents, we left the river behind us. Instead we found ourselves picking our way through quiet back-roads and picturesque country lanes. We'd planned our route carefully that morning, poring over the road map for some time to ensure that we passed a pub in good time for lunch.

The sky had clouded over and it had started to drizzle, so we were glad to see our pub almost exactly where we'd expected it to be. Not very surprising, you might think, but as G. pointed out once we were safely ensconced within, awaiting hot meals and with pints of bitter to hand, such things cannot be taken for granted.

"Right, you know when someone decides they want to publish a new map?"

"Oh yes, there's barely a morning goes by when I don't feel the primal urge to publish a new road map. I think it might be my sacred calling."

"As I was saying, there's not much to stop you from just copying someone else's is there? A little easier than slogging around measuring roads and lumping about theodolites and pointing at triangles on hills, or whatever it is that map-people do."

"Well, no, I suppose not. Can't say I'd given much thought to it."

"And of course," G. continued, "those chaps who have done all the slogging don't want other people cashing in on their hard work."

"That seems fair."

"So what the cunning devils do is throw in a few deliberate mistakes. That way, when a new map comes out, they can check it. If it has the same mistakes, it's obviously a copy."

"Ah! Right. That's rather clever."

"Quite. Anyway, my father was on a walking holiday, not too dissimilar to this one,

although without the higher purpose. He did it very well you understand. Planned every leg of the journey meticulously from the start."

"Very wise."

"Well yes, except that they spent four hours trying to have lunch in a pub that didn't exist. Marked on the map, but not in reality. Father was determined that they would follow the plan, and they walked up and down the same stretch of road for a good four or five hours, getting hungrier and hungrier. I think Father hoped that it would sort of just appear if they kept looking for long enough. They spent so long looking for it that it threw the entire plan for the rest of the holiday completely out of kilter, and they all got annoyed with each other and went home early. He's still not talking to one of them, and he hasn't trusted a map since."

ও

This fascinating tale, replete with human interest but rather lacking in purpose, was related over a rather smashing lunch. Eventually, I sat back with a sigh of contentment, looking up at the ceiling. A beam of sunlight shone through the window, creating a golden column of sparkling dust motes; each one gleaming as it danced and twirled through the glowing warmth.

"Gosh, isn't that pretty!" I said.

"Ugh!" B. exclaimed. "Just think, we're breathing that stuff in. A good job we can't see it most of the time or we'd all go around in gasmasks."

B. has never been one to appreciate the beauty of nature, and I told him so.

"Just think," I enthused, "imagine all the infinitesimal forces at work in that small space of air. Each tiny change in localised pressure, each flow and ebb of Brownian motion, each miniscule speck battered by thousands upon thousands of air molecules."

"Hah!" This outburst came not from B., but from a chap nursing a pint at the bar. I turned to look at him, but he was facing the bar with his back to me.

"And what about the molecules themselves, moved by electromagnetic and gravitational forces almost beyond our ability to comprehend," I continued.

"Hah!"

"Uh, I... um, yes. And then there're the sub-atomic forces, binding matter itself toge..."

"Hah!"

I turned angrily. "Right! What exactly, Sir, are you 'hah'ing at so derisively?"

He turned to face me. "It is my habit, Sir, to always deride those stupider than myself, and I always know when someone is stupider than me when they start harping on about poppycock like atoms and molecules."

"I beg your pardon?"

"It is clear that you have been taken in by the great delusion under which our society and civilisation labours, oppressing its peoples and retarding its development, and which I hope to see eradicated in future generations. The delusion of the atom!"

"But… but…" I floundered for words, failed, took a breath and started again. "I'm sorry, who are you?"

"My name is Dick Dorking, the world's first and foremost amolecularist. It is my intention to show people the ridiculous and infantile nature of atomic dogma."

I looked at G. and B. They looked at me and at each other. It was clear to us all that this fellow was clashing with only one cymbal. I turned back to him.

"Now look here my good fellow, of course atoms exist!"

"Have you ever seen one?"

"Well, not as such. Not just one by itself, no."

"Then how do you know they exist? Look…" He leant down till his eye was millimetres from the surface of the bar. "No matter how close I get, all I see is wood. No atoms or molecules."

"But they're too small to see with the naked eye."

"Hah! That's convenient. And what exactly is it that they're for?"

"What are atoms for? They… they're not *for* anything…"

"Then why bother with them?"

"Because scientists say that…"

"Hah! Scientists!"

"Now look," G. cut in. "We absolutely know that atoms and molecules exist. They've got electron microscopes nowadays so powerful that you can actually see individual molecules."

"Oh? And who's 'they'?"

"What? Um, scientists."

"Scientists again? Are any of you scientists?"

"No, not as such. I did an A-level though."

"Scientists! Wearing their silly robes and speaking their bizarre jargon, making sure that the whole thing remains an inaccessible mystery to the common man. Quoting books decades or centuries old that can have no possible relevance to modern everyday life. I tell you friends, that atoms are the opiate of the masses!"

Before any of us could rally ourselves for a response, he was off again.

"Now, a few years ago, it didn't really matter. People who believed in atoms could be looked down on as rather sad and pathetic, but basically harmless. I mean, if they really need to lean on this pseudo-scientific crutch, cuddle this ephemeral security blanket to get through the day, that's their lookout. It's just that those of us who are morally and intellectually stronger don't have any need for such things."

We all opened our mouths to answer but before any of us had even finished inhaling, he was off. Mr Dorking was obviously not a man to waste oratorical momentum.

"But then, they suddenly became dangerous. They said that they had 'split the atom'. They created weapons, bombs that could kill tens of thousands of people at once. Two whole cities were annihilated. Now, those of us who are rational, logical human beings must make a stand against fundamentalist atomisists and their Atom Delusion! I tell you, friends, that atomic theory has never brought anything but evil into the world."

G. had been holding his breath throughout this, and had gone slightly blue, but now he was ready with a reply before Dorking could recommence.

"Rubbish! Think of all the good it's done! Look at modern medicine and science. Look at the breakthroughs, the lives saved or changed for the better."

"True, but that has nothing to do with atoms or atomic theory. The whole thing is a fiction for the comfort of fools and the morally feeble."

"But..." It was too late, he thundered on with the momentum of a verbal steam-train.

"And it's all totally dependent on upbringing in any case!" he sneered. "You only believe in atoms and molecules because you were raised in a particular age and place. How many elements are there?"

"Um, a couple of hundred, I think, but I don't..."

"Hah! If you'd been born only three or four hundred years ago, you'd be swearing blind that there were only four! No, my friends, this whole sorry charade is only for the mentally feeble, a disease of the psyche which I soon hope to see cured."

This time, I got in with my response. "But it makes so much sense! Our understanding of the world depends on atomic theory. All of chemistry is based on the physical interactions of atoms and molecules, and all biology (and thus modern medicine) is based on chemistry."

"I neither know nor care about any of that."

"What?!" the three of us exclaimed together.

"You mean," said B. incredulously, "that you disbelieve in atoms, and dismiss atomic theory, but you've never studied physics?"

"I see no need to do so whatsoever. Do I need to have

studied palaeontology to know that dinosaurs never existed?"

We finished our drinks quickly, and did not bid him a good day.

Chapter 4

How religion has been used in the past for purposes for which it was never intended.

We had been walking onwards for nearly three hours, so by this point we were starting to feel quite hungry. The pub and its delicious lunches seemed a long way off, and I cast a wistful backwards look along the road.

I ran full tilt into the back of G., swayed back and, dragged by the weight of my backpack and tent, toppled over backwards. Now, what with the tent and bedroll, sleeping bag and cooking gear, spare undergarments and whatnots and other accumulated but vital apparatus, my backpack weighed rather more than my own somewhat spare frame, and I was left with my arms and legs in the air, flailing around like an upturned tortoise.

Now, I didn't know why G. had stopped. For all I knew, we'd just run into someone important, attractive or both. I flailed and kicked, which made the pans and things hanging off me rattle and clatter. B. kicked me in the ribs (not gently mind).

"Shut up and get off the floor! Have a look at this!"

"Disgusting is what it is!" said G.

I started rocking back and forth, and eventually created enough momentum to roll myself over onto my side. Now, instead of looking like a tortoise, I looked more like a cat that had found the fire, or possibly like a dead dog. From this relaxed position, I clambered laboriously to my feet.

G. and B. were staring up the road. A little area of it had been taped off, leaving just enough space for a car to get by.

"Look at that!" said B. sternly.

"Criminal, I call it," said G.

"What? What is it?" I asked, peering.

"Kids today. They can't see a surface without scrawling all over it can they?" G. said.

"If we'd done that in our youth, we'd have felt the sting of the corrective birch!" B. replied.

Looking past them, I could see that someone had been drawing on the road. It was a minimalist picture, elegant in its pure simplicity, pregnant with meaning and significance beyond the reach of my merely prosaic mind. Surrounded by a fence of tape bearing the slogan 'Police Line: Do Not Cross', was an outline of a human being in white pastels. Two police cars were parked near it on the far side, and a couple of policemen were standing nearby. One of them was writing in a notepad.

"I quite like it," I said. "Very indicative of the postmodernist thingummy."

My comrades pondered on this. "You may be right," G. conceded, something unprecedented in the history of the universe. "After all, a lot of graffiti is considered to be modern art nowadays."

"Yes, I like the fatalistic commentary on the busyness of everyday life, indicative of a man simply relaxing and lying down on a road, that symbol of modern, stressful living," B.

added.

"You don't think this is one of that Banksy chap's pieces do you?" I asked. "They can be worth quite a bit."

"I think I'd like to inspect the piece more closely," B. said. "I'm sure I can get us past the barrier. After all, I'm Press."

This wasn't really true. By 'Press', B. meant that he contributed the occasional article to the college magazine, which only got printed if they were having an especially slow month. However, he insisted that this technically made him a published writer and journalist. We never had the heart to tell him that the only reason any of his articles were published at all was because it was one of his friends who had been editor that year.

Before we could stop him, he was advancing towards the tape barrier. G. and I looked at each other, shrugged and followed. We caught up with B. just as he was ducking under the tape.

"Oi!" One of the policemen had spotted us and was advancing. "Get back there!"

"It's quite alright officer," B. explained. "I'm with the Press." He held up a little notebook and pencil as though it were inarguable proof. "Now, could you please tell us something about this work?"

"This what? Um, it'll be included in the press release for the local papers I suppose."

"Really? You're not going to be going national with this?"

"National? Um..." The bobby looked bewildered. "It was just a guy on the road..."

"Just a guy on the road!" B. exclaimed. "I beg to differ!"

"Oh, well, yes, I mean all life is precious," the peeler stammered. "I never meant 'just' a guy..."

"So you think that this is about life and death, yes? That's the deeper significance behind the work?"

"Significance? We're treating it as suspicious, but we already have the culprit, and he's confessed."

"I see." B. scribbled something in his notebook. "So what would you say this is worth?"

"Worth?"

"Yes, how much?" B. was relentless. He could really have been a journalist I think.

"Well, it wasn't premeditated, so I guess three or four years... I really don't know..."

"Years? I meant how much money!"

"Money? I suppose the family could sue the man but I'm not sure that..."

"Which man?"

"The one who committed the crime."

"You mean the artist?"

"Artist?"

"Yes."

"What?"

"What?"

Thankfully for the sanity of every person involved, the other chap, the one who had been writing in his notebook noticed us at this point.

"Here, put that down!"

All three of us jumped, and G. and I glanced at B., who was still holding his notepad and pencil.

"What?" asked B, rather flustered. "Why? Freedom of the Press and all that."

"Not you!" he snapped. He turned and pointed at G. instead. "You! Drop it!"

I turned to see what G. was holding, half expecting to see

that he had pulled a gun from somewhere and was preparing to sell his life dearly. Instead, he was holding his walking stick. No simple crook was this but one of those good old-fashioned, sturdy thumbsticks with the little Y-shape at the end and a leather loop to go over the wrist. G. claims that it is an alpenstock that he made in Switzerland with the Scouts. I suspect that it cost him ten pounds in a Devonshire newsagents.

"Um, why?" he asked, obviously puzzled.

"Why? It's a dangerous weapon is why! Carrying an offensive weapon is against the law in case you didn't know," the policeman added sarcastically. I began to dislike him.

"A dangerous weapon?" I sneered. "It's a stick! I could arm myself like that in thirty seconds by wandering over to the nearest tree!"

He surveyed me soberly. "I suggest you don't try it, Sir. I'll have you arrested if you do."

"Now look here," G. started, reasonably, "this is not a weapon. A weapon is an object designed for the purpose of killing or wounding a fellow creature. This is designed for the purpose of bearing me up when I grow weary. We're hiking you see."

"Hah! That's a very old one. That's ended in murder before now."

I glanced at the outline on the road and wondered if I was viewing the aftermath of an alpenstock-related slaying. The policeman saw my look and nodded knowingly.

"Oh yes. You're looking at the end of the story right there!"

He began to tell us all about it. Rather than offend you with the dreary policeman's details, I shall give you the simple gist of it. What happened is this: A chap had decided to go on a long trip and was going by foot. I imagine it was a pilgrimage not dissimilar to our own, albeit longer and involving a lot more cross-country stuff. Now, the journey was going to be rather arduous as well as long because he was one of those outward-bound survivalist types. Instead of taking the roads and using bridges like a sensible chap, he was going to cut straight across country whenever he could. He was expecting to have to climb hills and ford rivers, and face the real possibility of fending off angry farmers' dogs since his journey would have by necessity involved a small amount of trespass.

Knowing about this journey, a very good friend of the man gave the fellow a present. He gave him a walking staff. Not just a walking stick mind, but a proper staff, solid and stout and capable of supporting him up steep slopes, and holding him up when fording fast-flowing rivers and even of beating off the dogs of angry farmers if needs be. A good, practical and well-thought gift.

So this bloke set off on his journey and, true to form, it was indeed long and hard and arduous, and involved steep hills and deep, fast-flowing rivers. The walking staff was a great help and bore him up, and supported him when he needed it, and protected him from man and beast. And all was good.

Eventually, he ended up travelling along a road, and met another traveller moving in the same direction. They hiked along together for a while, and as they walked they chatted. They got on alright, and all was well. However, the tale took a nasty turn. As they talked, they began to disagree on certain fundamental issues. The conversation became heated; they bickered; they argued. The argument grew into a blazing row. In a fit of passion, the man took his staff and beat his fellow hiker to death with it.

"The man instantly regretted his decision, phoned us on his mobile and waited for us to arrive," the policeman concluded. "He's being driven back to the station as we speak. Now, are you sure you don't want to put that stick down?"

"If it's all the same to you," G. said after a moment's thought, "I think I'll keep hold of it."

Chapter 5

Evolution and religion. How Christianity
is unnatural, and therefore good.

We walked along in silent contemplation of this interesting
little lesson, and thus, I thought, showing a proper
pilgrimatical spirit. Very pious and proper and whatnot. We
reached the top of a ridge, and found ourselves looking up at
a line of low hills. I'd like to identify them for you; tell you
where to find them on a map, but I'm afraid I can't. My grasp
of geography is on a similar par to my grasp of theology,
small, but very slowly growing with every step I take along
the road. They were, I thought, possibly the Pennines. I
voiced this opinion, and was told, somewhat scornfully, by G.
that we were nowhere near the Pennines, and that I should
stop being such a silly ass.

On top of those low hills, we could see shapes. Tall,
ominous sorts of shapes, as though the Martians had arrived
in their tripods and were enjoying the view before they turned
on the heat-rays. They were windmills. A wind-farm, if you
can credit such a thing. A quote sprang to mind about sowing
the breeze and reaping the whirlwind. Shakespeare, or one of
that crowd.

"Ugh!" said B. "Hideous aren't they?"

"Oh no," said G. as deadpan as you like. "I think they complement the landscape perfectly!"

"What?" we both cried in indignant outrage. G. looked at us.

"That was sarcasm wasn't it?" I ventured.

"Oh no. I'm never sarcastic. Ever."

"Humph," said B. "Well they are hideous, even if you don't say that they might not be, even when you don't mean it. Ugly. Unnatural."

With that, we walked on. I had got out the map and was trying to find the Pennines when G. muttered something.

"Beg pardon old thing?"

"I said 'unnatural'. I've been thinking."

The problem with G. is that all his thinking is done under cover. B. has the previously documented grinding noise and metallic smell, but all of G.'s thinking is done inside his own head. A recipe for headaches and conditions in later life I call it.

"And what," I enquired, "has the old cerebral blancmange been wobbling over now?"

"It seems to me that the question of whether or not things are natural is quite an important one, and that we need to determine whether or not the term 'natural' has an intrinsic moral value."

I blinked. B. would never have come out with something like that. He would have complained about his feet. I opened my mouth to reply, and paused, uncertain how to proceed. I furrowed the old brow. I gave the statement some adamantine-hard thought.

"Um… what?"

"Well, B. was saying that the windmills were unnatural, as though that were automatically a bad thing."

"What are you saying about me?" interrupted B. "How far's the campsite now, eh? Is it a long way?"

"Hang on there," I said, still trying to catch up. "Is this going to be about progress and industry and so forth?" G. is involved in industry you see, at some level anyway. I'm not too sure how because he's never seemed particularly industrious to me.

"Not at all. I am actually thinking about the homosexual problem."

I blinked again. "The who-how?"

"The homosexual problem."

"Are they?"

"Are they what?"

"A problem?"

"Oh no. Well, not to me anyway. But generally. Theologically speaking, since we are now trying to speak theologically."

"Um…" I was lost again, "…sorry?"

"Look," he began, "somewhere in the Bible, it says something about men not lying with men."

"Yes, top ten commandments isn't it? Don't bare false witnesses or something. 'Lying: V. bad.'"

"No, as in sleeping with them. The old carnal act."

"Although," B. chipped in, "it says nothing about women lying with women, so that video you kept watching back in uni is probably al…"

"Shut up, B." I said firmly. "Now."

"But anyway, to support the biblical injunction, people trot out stuff about homosexuality being unnatural."

"Right, are we talking about those penguins now? The ones in Berlin? Because Berlin is not natural. It was built by ancient Germans, using artificial means."

"No, I am not talking about gay German penguins!"

"Good. Just checking."

"Now, I'm not well read, as a Christian. I'm not even sure I am one. I agree that this pilgrimage is a good idea, but I'm still holding the thing at arm's length so as to get a good look at it, if you see what I mean? You're the one who actually read that pamphlet, and got us talking about mortal sin and all the rest of it."

"Yes, well sorry about that. It seemed a good idea at the time and I…"

"Don't apologise. Anyway, it seems to me that all those sins are very natural. It seems to me that if you take the evolutionary theory as being the best, and compatible with most of the rest of it, then everything that is described as a sin is simply us acting upon our natural instincts, as they have developed out of necessity in our bestial past."

My brain reeled. A lot of lengthy words in there! I noticed that B. wasn't even trying. He was instead trying to affect a limp in the hope that we would call a pause for a little while. I was too interested in G.'s theorising, to be honest. G. is an intelligent sort of a chap, but he doesn't often show it. More often he is interested in a quiet pipe and a glass of port in our club, or in coddling Monty. Now, however, his brain was clearly going at ten to the gallon.

"So what you're saying then is…?"

"What Christians appear to be asked to do is to act in an unnatural manner. They are told to act in a way opposite to their natural inclinations."

"What, 'O sinful man' sort of thing. Original sin and all the rest?"

"Hmm. Original sin in the sense that what Christians refer to as sins are hang-overs from our origins as lesser animals.

We have evolved to an extent where we recognise that those urges that were suitable for ensuring the successful passage of our DNA to the next generation are no longer suitable for us as truly sentient and potentially spiritual creatures."

"My feet hurt," said B. "Can we stop?"

"In a bit," I promised. "But first G. has to get himself out of this knot he's wrapping himself up in."

"But they *hurt*!"

"No. Press on. March on to victory and all that. Slog on. Onwards and upwards, forwards and out. Half a league, half a…"

"If I keep walking, will you stop encouraging me?"

"Yes."

"Thank you." He plodded onwards.

"Anyway," G. said, "it seems to me that now, possibly even as a furtherance of our evolution, people are being asked to cast off the remnants of that bestial phase of our development as a species. If an animal finds a huge amount of food, it will eat to excess by instinct since it may not get another chance to feed for a while. Similarly, most animals will mate as often as is practical, with as many mates as is practical. Not out of a conscious need to pass on its genes, but out of instinct. This is how we have evolved."

"So you're saying that our natural inclination, going back to the time of the dinosaurs, is to be lecherous pigs?"

"Absolutely. But now we are told, and not just Christians, but most religions, that we are to ignore those primal urges that ensured the survival of our ancestors. Instead of only looking out for ourselves, and only feeding our young, and sleeping with as many mates as possible, we are told to share all we have, love each other unconditionally, restrict ourselves strictly to a single mate, through thick and thin. I tell you that Christianity is utterly unnatural, and, all that being so, it is still not a bad thing."

"Well yes then. Fair enough and point made. So where do the homosexuals come in?"

"They don't really. I was just trying to demonstrate that from a religious perspective, arguing that something is 'unnatural' is a bit of a dead end. Also, the argument rather neatly gets round the question of the kind of God that would give you sexual urges and taste-buds and whatnot and then tell you not to use them."

"Um," I was getting lost again, just when I thought I'd caught up. "But surely He still did that, in a roundabout way?"

"Not at all. He simply set in motion evolutionary processes that resulted, intentionally or otherwise, in us."

"Even B.?"

G. paused. "Well, perhaps not B. He might very well be the work of the *other side*."

"Am I being talked about again? Are we nearly there? We're going to stop in this county aren't we? My feet *hurt!*"

We chose to ignore this. "God set up the whole evolutionary system," G. continued, "and to survive within that system, we evolved with all those urges, needs and desires. Now that we have, again intentionally or otherwise on His part, graduated from that phase of our development, we are instructed to resist those desires, to cast off the things of our racial youth."

"All true and well-reasoned, but only if you follow the theory of evolution, as opposed to the biblical stuff. Genesis and so forth."

"Yes, but I do."

"Ah. Right ho then. So all's natural and good? Unnatural

and good, in fact."

"Ah yes, good point. After all, look at Monty. He's perfectly natural and utterly disgusting."

G. glared at me, while Montgomery looked me with an expression of hurt reproach. He had been trotting along quite quietly, but now he slunk off with a sullen look in his eye, as though determined to live up to this reputation that he had somehow acquired.

"Right. So what you're arguing, coming around full circle as it were, is that because some people claim that homosexuality is unnatural, it must therefore be a good thing, just like Christianity."

"Yes. No wait, no. Um, not that Christianity is necessarily good. Not that it isn't. Um... I'm getting confused now."

"My feet *really* hurt! Let's sit down now!" said B.

"Look," said G., rallying. "I have no problem with homosexuality. Not for me, but each to their own. What I was trying to demonstrate was that it was nonsensical to refer to it as 'unnatural', in terms of using the word in a derogatory way, since the same is true, if not more so, of Christianity."

A scream came from a nearby field, followed by Monty. In his mouth was what looked suspiciously like a bra. After a couple of seconds, an extremely red-faced young man appeared. Red-faced, not with embarrassment, I might add, but with a quite remarkable rage. He was followed by a red-faced young woman (although she looked rather less cross and much more embarrassed).

"What the devil are you doing!?" the young chap said with no little volume of voice. "A vicious, nasty brute like that should be kept muzzled and tied up indoors!"

"Oh, it's quite alright," G. assured him. "He's completely natural."

Chapter 6

On Christian perfection.

That night, it being a pleasant sort of night, and since we weren't especially close to any convenient B&Bs, we pitched our tents and camped.

Now, you'll never find me advocating the great outdoors in favour of the greater indoors, but there is something special about camping. When it's dry. And warm. There's nothing special about being cold and wet and getting trench-foot in your hands.

But when it is nice, and you've got a few bottles of beer with you (real ale that is, not that horrible watery lager stuff), and you can make a little fire (with about four entire fire-lighters, half a box of matches and an inordinate amount of swearing), nothing can quite beat camping.

Once the swearing and so forth were completed, we sat around our little fire, drinking our bottled beer and staring contemplatively into the flickering flames. Well, I was. I can't vouch for the other two. I doubt B. even contemplates contemplatively.

There was silence, broken only by the murmur of the breeze in the nearby trees, and the snap and crackle of our fire, sending flittering shadows running over everything its light touched. It was a moment of peace and stillness, of tranquillity and calm. The kind of moment in which you can almost feel something moving over you, a vast and comforting presence, beyond the senses but still palpable and real, too far to reach but near enough to touch. A moment of deep and silent poetry.

"I say," said B. "Hasn't it gone quiet?"

And that was that, the moment was ruined. I expected that he was going to start talking about the football results. Not that B. cares for football, but he can rarely think of anything else to talk about when he isn't complaining about something, so he keeps abreast of them.

"I reckon," he began unpromisingly, "that there isn't a single Christian alive who isn't an enormous hypocrite."

The lack of speculation on Everton's new scrum-half or whatever the devil it is that they're called caught me off-guard, so it took a second to muster a decent response.

"That's not fair," I said. "There've got to be a few good ones. I met the local vicar a few times and he seemed alrightish."

"No. None of them practice what they preach though do they?"

"Well, pretty much," said G. "Most of them anyway."

"Not at all!" retorted B., warming to his subject. "All a bunch of hypocrites! They say that you should be perfect, even as God is perfect. I'm not aware of any perfect Christians, are you?"

"Not now you mention it, no," I conceded. "Some pretty good ones, but no perfect ones at all."

"See? Hypocrites!"

"I remember in my younger days thinking that Pamela Anderson was rather perfect," G. said. "I'm not sure she was a Christian though. I'm not sure they're allowed to run around beaches with that little on to be honest."

"I'm not entirely sure that that was the perfection that B. was driving at, and I'm entirely sure that it's not the perfection the Bible was driving at. I don't think that God looks like Pamela Anderson in her Baywatch days."

"How do you know?"

"Well, it… stands to reason doesn't it? He's intangible, and ineffable and whatnot."

"And Pamela Anderson was extremely effable!" B. chipped in.

"Don't be rude," I admonished. "You brought this subject up, now you have to help maintain the tone."

"Point still stands though," he sniffed sulkily. "No perfect Christians, therefore they're hypocrites."

"Well perhaps it's the attempt, rather than the achievement that counts," I suggested.

"The way I see it," G. said, opening another bottle of beer, "is that it's like a maths test."

I frowned at this. "Liable to give you a nosebleed you mean?"

"Pardon?"

"A maths exam gave me a nosebleed. Actually, it might have been a physics paper, but it was the mathematics involved that burst the blood vessel."

"I see. No, I don't mean it'll give you a nosebleed."

I nodded. This was good. I don't like nosebleeds, and it sent me into an awful panic at the time, and quite threw me off my physics. I blame that loss of blood for my poor mark to this day. I have no idea what the unfortunate marker thought when he opened the paper to find a Rorschach-test smear of my nasal gore in double-exposure on the inside of the test. I hope he didn't dock me marks for it, but he probably did. Physics teachers are like that. If it had been a biology paper I would probably have been given bonus marks.

"In maths papers, you get marks for the right answer, but you also get marks for the working out."

I nodded. "That's true. The same goes for physics as well."

"And it seems to me that the same is true of morality. You get marks for doing the right thing, but you also get marks for doing it for the right reasons."

"The ends justify the means sort of thing?"

"I suppose so, yes. If you do the right thing for the right reasons, then it's all good. But if you do the wrong thing for the right reasons, that's got to be worth something surely?"

"I suppose... But presumably the other way round is not so good? Doing the right thing for the wrong reason?"

By this point B. was starting to look a little lost. "So if I saved a baby from a burning building, but was trying to kidnap it, that would be worse than if I kidnapped it to save it from burning?"

G. and I looked at each other. "Umm..." I replied, my brain going ten-to-the-dozen, "yes, I think so."

G. nodded slowly, trying to catch up. How does this happen? G. and I are both considerably brighter than solid old B., but nonetheless sometimes the old fellow bowls us a queer ball and we both fall over trying to grasp it.

"Anyway," G. continued, rallying remarkably, "the point is that no, Christians are not perfect, and probably can't be."

I shook my head. "Actually, I'm sure I read someone somewhere saying that he had met one old woman who was a perfect Christian."

"Was it before the sixties?"

"Oh yes. Back in the eighteenth century I think."

"Doesn't count then. They didn't have nearly so many sins to contend with back in the olden days. All three of us would have been fine if we'd only been born two or three hundred years earlier."

"Ah. Fair enough. No sex, drugs etc and so forth."

"Indeed not. Well, there must have been some sex for us to have been here at all. No drugs though. Oh, except opium and such-like. Anyway," he tried again, "I reckon that it is the attempt for perfection, rather than the attainment that is the thing. After all, if you aim high and fail, you're still doing better than someone who aims low and succeeds."

"But they're still hypocrites," B. asserted stoutly.

"Yes, they are. But I'm not sure that in this case that's necessarily a bad thing."

"Very true." I added. "Just think how utterly insufferable they would be if they *were* perfect!"

Chapter 7

How each religion sees part of the elephant, or would do if it weren't for Health & Safety.

At this point, I put my hand down to pick up my beer from where I had left it on the floor. Instead, I encountered something hairy and warm. Now, my beer wasn't perhaps as chilled as I'd have liked, but it most definitely was not hairy!

I recoiled with a yell and Monty looked up, ears back and eyes wide. He curled a lip at me and went back to lapping up my beer.

"G. if you aren't careful, that dog is going to end up in the flames *before* he dies as well as afterwards."

"Well, the little chap's got to drink hasn't he? He needs a nice beer as much as the rest of us."

"Dogs should not drink beer. I'm pretty sure that's in the Bible somewhere."

"I'm not sure it is you know."

"Actually," B. piped up, "there's something about not wasting on the dogs what's meant for the children."

"Yes, but children shouldn't drink beer either."

"Aha, but in the old days, the water was poisonous, so they had to drink beer all the time."

I turned to G. "I thought you said the old days weren't so sinful. I hardly see how that was the case if everyone was from toddlers to dodderers was roaring drunk!"

"Ah, but the children in those days only drank small beer."

"What's small beer?"

B. snorted. "Even I know that! It's beer that only comes in half pints."

G. and I paused and looked at each other. "Yes B.," G. said consolingly. "That's quite right. Now drink up, there's a good fellow."

"The point still stands," I forged on, fixing a glowering eye upon G., "that your wretched hound has stolen my beer. He's a creature of unmitigated sin and devilment, an engine of wickedness and evil sent to plague me and my poor ale bottle."

Monty looked up and wagged his tail at this shining endorsement of his skills.

G., however, was not so appreciative. "He is not!" he cried, sweeping Monty up protectively. "He's just misunderstood. He's a delicate soul, trying to find his place in a harsh and unforgiving universe that is yet to recognise his true talents and potential."

"His talents are well known!" I replied hotly. "They include chasing innocent cats, knocking over little old ladies, howling at the moon at 3am on a Monday morning, biting the ankles of all and sundry, and more recently, pilfering lingerie and stealing good beer! As to his potential, I see in him all the makings of a second-rate pair of fur gloves, or a very mangy hat!"

"No!" G. yelped, hugging the hound closer to him. I've never quite been able to figure out G's attitude to Monty. As a father, G. is a little distant, but strict and stern in the fashion of the old school. Very much a 'Broth without Bread' sort of a parent is old G. However, when it comes to his ratty little canine, all the doting and warmth that he keeps locked up (except presumably for Mrs G., at least a couple of times) he expends on Montgomery.

"This," said B., rumbling into motion, "is like those blind chaps."

The burgeoning argument was abruptly aborted. We both stared at him.

"Pardon?"

"Oh you know, the blind chaps. I was just thinking how funny it was how the two of you look at Monty and see completely different things."

"Not at all. G. can see perfectly well what Monty is, he just refuses to accept it."

"Not at all. J. knows in his heart of hearts that Monty's a good boy, but his envy of my dog-raising abilities chokes him."

We glared at each other. B. cleared his throat uncomfortably.

"Yes, well, that's all good I suppose, friendly disagreement and all that. But that's sort of what happened to the blind chaps."

"Which blind chaps?"

"The ones in the zoo. Oh, you know!"

"B.," I said firmly, "even in these brutal and uncaring times, we have not yet reached the point of keeping our infirm and disabled in zoos. Even in the good old days, they were allowed to tour around the place, to be stared at by different fellows every week. To keep them confined in one place for any amount time would be inhumane."

"Oh no, they weren't kept at the zoo. No, they were just visiting."

"I am, no doubt, going to sound rather heartless," G. put in, "but how much benefit can the sight-impaired derive from going to a zoo?"

"Ah, but that's the clever bit! They were allowed into the cages to touch the animals."

"Touch the animals!" I cried.

"Oh yes. They went to have a good old feel of an elephant you see."

"Preposterous," I said.

"Ridiculous!" G. exclaimed.

"Unthinkable," I added.

"Quite impossible," G. replied.

"Really? Oh. Why so?"

"Well, health and safety of course! They'd never let a trio of blind chaps into an enclosure with a potentially dangerous animal!"

"Absolutely!" G. chimed in. "The poor pachyderm would see three small, blind creatures and assume they were mice! Having no carving knife to hand, it would go on a rampage, most likely killing or seriously injuring one or all of the blind fellows!"

"But it's supposed to show how different faiths and denominations can..."

"Don't you clutter up your head with that sort of balderdash," I cautioned. "It wouldn't be allowed and that's final."

Personally, I was worried about B. I thought that he was on the verge of saying something profound and thought-provoking, and was determined to put a stop to it before he did himself serious harm. Obviously that perfidious canine-lover G. had had similar thoughts, and the enemy of my enemy is my friend, beer-stealing mutts notwithstanding.

"My dear fellow," I continued more gently, "I see where you're going with this, but God clearly isn't an elephant."

"Unless you're a Hindu!" G. butted in.

"Yes, quite. Unless you're a Hindu, in which case your god might very well be an elephant, or at least a being of elephantine appearance."

"Why not? Why can't God be an elephant?"

"Because he doesn't have a trunk. I tell you that in these days of stringent health and safety precautions, such an analogy is entirely unworkable. It's a lawsuit waiting to happen. Besides, if God were just an elephant which we were seeing piecemeal, you have to ask yourself, who is staring at the buttocks?"

He didn't have an answer to this, and since Monty had by this point spilled all the beer while we were involved in our debate, we soon went to bed.

Chapter 8

How people, having rejected traditional religions, find a gap in their lives, and how they find substitutes that are not replacements.

The next morning, we woke and cooked breakfast. As I poked and prodded at the sausages singularly failing to cook over the little gas stove, I glowered at Monty. The little hell-hound was showing far too much interest in my breakfast for my liking.

B. climbed gracelessly out of his tent. It was like watching a very large mole scrambling out of an enormous red molehill. He peered lustfully at my sausages.

"Aha! Breakfast!"

"Indeed. Although we'll be eating them raw at this rate. This is where we get to the deprivations bit of the pilgrimage. Raw sausages and tea made with teabags and long-life milk. Ugh!"

At this point a very dishevelled-looking G. poked his head through the door of his tent. G. normally puts so much time into looking shevelled that to see him otherwise was quite a shock, and I nearly dropped the frying pan.

"Egad! Look what the cat dragged through a bush

backwards!"

"Oh shut up! Nobody's at their best after a night in a tent!"

"I bet Red Indians are!" B. piped in.

"You can't call them that anymore," I scolded. "You've got to call them Amerinjuns!"

"The point is that I have fallen from my usual peaks of grace, and it will take a shower and a stiff cup of tea to return me to my former heights!"

"That was it!" B. cried snapping his fingers. "I was going to ask you something last night, but what with dogs and elephants, I forgot."

G. and I looked at each other warily. B.'s mind had lurched into gear, and who knew where that terrible engine would drag us?

"It's all very well dragging us off around the countryside on this pilgrimage of yours, but how do we know we're on the right track?"

I can't honestly say I liked B.'s tone. A touch churlish you might say. "Hang on," I said sharply, "when did this become 'my' pilgrimage? You agreed you were quite as bad as me. In fact you claimed, much to my scorn I might add, that you were even worse than me, which is frankly laughable. So no more of this tosh about 'my' pilgrimage! And I know we're on the right track, because the road sign said B3472 and, according to the old OS, that is precisely the track upon which we need to be."

"No, no, no, I don't mean the right road. It's all very well saying how bad we are, and I think I may have overestimated my own case incidentally, but how do we know that we wouldn't have been just as well sticking up a dream-catcher and doing some cross-legged humming?"

G. had been rummaging in his tent for a hairbrush, which he had not found judging by his state as his head popped out like the birth of a very keen baby. "B.," he inquired fiercely, "are you implying that we should have gone... New Age?"

"Well right now it seems a darned sight more sensible than sitting in tents on a freezing cold morning, failing to eat sausages. We could have been safe and warm and doing things with crystals."

"Well I think it's all poppycock!" I declared stoutly. "Absolute nonsense. A mish-mash of cultural leavings with no kind of ethos or authority."

"A mish-mash," G. popped out again, "like a middle-eastern religious sect given authority by an extinct empire and with anglicised nomenclature?"

"Well quite. Wait, no. That's different! That does have an ethos and authority. Even if it's Roman. As soon as someone can point out a Native American Empire, I'll start taking dream-catchers more seriously."

"Well, all that aside," B. said after a pause, "the stove has gone out."

I looked down and expressed my surprise and annoyance in a succinct and emphatic manner, disturbing a flock of starlings that flew up with a great whirr of wings.

"Um, chaps," I said tentatively, "I think breakfast's a non-starter."

"Breakfast," declared G., "is the most important meal of the day. A day without breakfast goes downhill from thereon in."

B. stared mournfully at the pink, floppy sausages. Monty stared wistfully at them. I glared at them hatefully, cause of all my current worldly woes as they were. Those two sausages represented everything wrong about the world, pink and unfinished, ruined before they had started. Where could I turn to gain surcease from my sausage-shaped troubles?

"I say!" G. once more emerged, like a partly-groomed jack-in-the-box, OS in hand. "There's a fast-food place just down the road. That'll do!"

"Fast food is very rarely either," I said firmly, standing up and taking a couple of paces about our little camp. "We are not quite that badly off are we? I can relight the stove. We can still have sausages!" You see how my heroic spirit reasserted itself, even when faced with the most ferocious and insurmountable of problems? I'm like that you see. Unconquerable.

"'fraid not J.," B. pointed behind me. "Look."

I turned very slowly. Monty looked up at me, his tail wagging. Then he saw the expression on my face and his tail dropped. He swallowed quickly, turned tail and fled into G.'s tent, and that was the end of the sausages.

An hour later saw us safely ensconced in an eatery of dubious renown. A Mctuckey King or some-such. You know the sort. Pedlars of unsustaining but momentarily satisfying culinary dross. I was chewing most contentedly on the food-like substance that made up my breakfast. It might not have been stove-cooked sausages, but I have to admit that the warm indoors and the tables and chairs made the wet grass and bracing breeze of our camp practically uncivilised.

Conversation had ceased as we tucked into the fare, when suddenly a shadow fell over us. I fancied that a cloud had passed over the sun, and turned to glance out of the window. I almost choked on my burger.

I am not, I hope, a cruel man, nor a man given over to pointing out the shortcomings of other humans beings, especially when they were as obvious as this poor young woman. She was, in a word, fat, but fat is a very small word to describe an awfully large woman. It is like using 'big' to describe the universe. Technically it is true, but much more could be said.

I am of course gifted with a rather good figure. Svelte you might say. Sleek. Thus one might think that I am given to judge the severely overweight a little too harshly. Be that as it may, this young woman was vast. I shall not labour the point.

She edged through the doors and advanced on the counter. I saw that B. and G. had been similarly awestruck by this considerable young lady. She ordered enough food to feed all three of us for the rest of the pilgrimage then looked around for somewhere to sit.

She noticed that we were staring. As one, we turned away, faces red. We stared at our food, not daring to meet each other's eyes. Then, I saw a ripple in my tea. Followed by another, more noticeable one. Then a third, even more pronounced. I looked up to see the lady advancing on our position.

"What were you looking at?" she demanded.

We all looked at each other. "Ah, ah, ah, well…" I said.

The others nodded in agreement.

"Look, it's a medical condition, okay?" she snapped.

"Oh, wh-wh-what? What is? A medical condition?" I made a great show of looking her up and down.

"Yes! And I'm rather sensitive about it, all right?"

B. nodded knowingly. "Ah, the old thyroids eh? My aunt suffered terribly from having a thyroid."

The girl sat heavily next to me and I thought for a moment

that I would be catapulted into the ceiling, but it seems that fast-food benches are made of stern stuff. Perhaps they get a lot of generously proportioned customers.

"It's nothing to do with that! I can't feel hungry."

We thought about this for a second. "Surely," G. ventured after a moment, "you mean that you can't feel full? You don't know when to stop?"

She shook her head. "Nope. Well, that too. I have a numb stomach. But the real problem is that I can't feel hungry. I found out five years ago. I wasn't eating anything. I almost starved to death. I looked like a skeleton."

I stared hard at her face and tried to imagine it. I failed.

"I very nearly died," she said solemnly. "But the doctors figured out what the problem was. So now I have to eat just in case. I'm never sure when I need food, and how much, so I just take on as much as I can. Anything and everything." She smacked her lips. "And now I'm in no danger of starving to death ever again!"

"Isn't modern medicine wonderful?" I replied weakly.

"Oh yes, I...Ooh! My food's ready! Nice talking to you. Bye!"

She jumped up (no really, she did, it was magnificent in a bizarre way) and hurried over to the counter with a Richter-scale tread to collect her meal.

Suddenly not feeling so hungry, we got up and left quietly, and were soon on our way.

Chapter 9

***If so many people have all experienced
God, surely there must be something
there to experience, even if the
description isn't always the same.***

We had been walking for some two hours or so, and were
well into our stride when we drew near to a village. I forget
its exact name, but I fancy it was one of the Parvas, or
possibly a Magna. It's isn't actually very important to be
honest. As I say, we were approaching this fine little place
when a car came rushing down at us like a greased bluebottle
and we had to dive onto the verges to avoid being run down.

The car came to a screeching stop and we turned to give
our solemn opinion to the driver regarding his proficiency
with a car. I had a particularly cutting and vinegared barb to
hurl, but all of our abuses were cut short when he wound
down the window, leaned out and yelled, "Run! Dinosaur!"

He then put his foot down and went speeding off again.
After a few second's worth of open-mouthed silence, we
glanced at each other. G. offered a weak smile. I returned it,
and gave a little 'aha!' laugh. B. chuckled feebly. I shook my
head and tutted, smiling. G. nodded at me and gave a grin. G.
chuckled a little more heartily.

"A dinosaur…" I murmured.

"How absurd," G. said.

"How silly," B. remarked.

"What a foolish joke," I said. "A dinosaur."

"Does he think we're idiots?" G. asked.

We turned and continued along the road, still chuckling to ourselves. The mirth had all but died down when another car went zooming past us. The driver didn't bother to stop, instead contenting herself with winding down the window.

"No! Turn round and run for your lives!" she yelled as she whizzed by. "It's a great brown thing!"

We frowned at each other. Then shook our heads again and smiled.

"You've got to give them marks for effort," G. said.

"Obviously not much in the way of television signal in these parts," I commented. "Making their own entertainment in the tradition of the good old days."

We all nodded and continued our walk towards the Parva or Magna, each quietly musing bemusedly and amusedly at the quaint trick that some locals had attempted to pull on us. We carried on for some minutes when a couple came zooming round a corner towards us on bicycles.

"Flee! Dinosaur!" the man shrieked as he passed.

"Save yourselves!" the woman added, pedalling furiously.

G., B. and I stared after them. I put my hands on my hips. "This is beginning to wear a little thin! A joke's a joke, but really!"

"Sad, I call it," G. sniffed contemptuously. "Rather pathetic."

"Yes…" said B. doubtfully. "You don't… you don't suppose there's anything in it do you?"

"Oh come now, B.," I began but he cut me off.

"Not about it being a dinosaur," he added hastily, "but something similarish."

"Similarish to a dinosaur? A dragon perhaps?"

B. went a little red. "Don't give me that," he snapped. "If one person tells me they've seen a dinosaur, I call 'em a crank. If two people tell me they've seen a dinosaur, I assume it's a joke. But four?"

"Is still clearly a joke," G. said firmly. "It'll take far more than two motorists and a pair of cyclists to convince me of dinosaurs or dinosaur-like creatures in southern England."

At this precise moment, and with admirable comic timing, a huge crowd of people rounded the corner ahead, running in a wild and headlong stampede straight towards the three of us, bearing down like so many alarmed wildebeest. Not that I've ever been charged by stampeding wildebeests you understand, but I'm sure that the impression is very similar. All wide, rolling eyes and stamping feet.

The three of us were obliged to step up onto the verge as the horde came careering past us. It was composed of all sorts of people, young and old together, all hurrying upon their terrified way. One of the last to pass was a teenage boy who saw us, taking in our rucksacks and sleeping rolls.

"Don't go that way!" he called to us, slowing his flight. "There's a huge green monster! It's rampaging down the high street!" And then he was gone, following the rest of the herd in its headlong dash.

We continued to stand on the verge, staring after them for some minutes without comment. We stole furtive glances up the road in the direction we were travelling, none of us willing to admit that we were giving the slightest credence to this ridiculous notion, but neither willing to be taken by surprise by a Tyrannosaurus Rex on the loose.

"You noticed of course," said G. with a superior curl of his lip," that they can't even get their story straight. One of them has said that this supposed beast is green, the other has said it is brown."

"Perhaps, it's greenish brown," I ventured.

"Or brownish green," B. added.

"Nonsense! The fact that they can't even decide what this alleged creature is like merely adds to my conviction that this is nothing more than a hoax, or at best a mass hallucination."

In the distance we heard a noise. I wouldn't swear that it was a roar. It could have been a motorcycle engine, or someone dropping a load of boxes, or a shutter door being pulled down. It could have been any one of these things. We all glanced at each other furtively to see if the others had heard it and thought the same things.

"You know…" I began, "we could go back a bit and take the right turn…"

G. and B. looked at each other, both waiting for the other to agree with me so that they could be outvoted and forced not to go through the primordially infested village. Neither were willing to give in though.

"Nonsense," G said reluctantly. "Dinosaurs have been extinct for millions of years. The odds of one rampaging through rural England are slender at best."

"Yes, of course," B. replied miserably. "Utter drivel. Just a silly prank. A very well-organised, realistic-seeming prank."

"Ah, yes," I nodded. "You're both right of course… I suppose." With this rationale firmly in place, we took our lives in our hands and trudged towards the Parva.

The village in question was only quarter of an hour's walk or so from our previous position, and we soon encountered the 'You are Now Entering' sign, all of us with nerves ajangle, each looking to our flanks, wary of the method of attack favoured by the common Velociraptor Mongoliensis. No such creatures emerged from the hedgerows however, as we made our entry into the settlement.

All seemed well, and there were no signs of passing sauropods as we approached a crossroads that seemed to mark the centre of the place, complete with a quaint little village green.

"Of course, I was confident all along that it was just a complex hoax," G. declared. "If there really was a dinosaur, then why haven't we seen any evidence of it eh? It doesn't matter how many people tell you that a thing is true, a rational man must stick solidly to the evidence of his own senses!"

I nodded absent-mindedly, not really listening. I was staring in a kind of trance at the three-toed footprint in the soft turf of the green. A footprint that could not have measured less than three feet long.

B. hadn't noticed, gazing apprehensively as he was around the green. "Good God Almighty!" he yelped. "Take a look at that!"

We looked, and saw a pile of what decency must restrict me to referring to as manure. 'Pile' is perhaps too small a word for this mighty and Himalayan mound of ordure. It does not capture its gravitas and silent, solid, steaming majesty. Such a heap as could have been seen, and most likely smelled, from space.

G. gave a snort of disbelief and started towards it, with God knows what end in mind, but he was stopped when he stepped in the footprint I had been examining and promptly tripped over.

He picked himself up hurriedly, and glared at B. and me, as though daring us to have noticed. I smiled innocently at him and, after a brief glower, he turned to see what he had caught his foot in. I saw the colour momentarily drain from his face.

"Ahem," he said quietly, swallowing. "Yes... well, a village full of people prepared to play such an elaborate trick on a group of travellers is clearly no place for decent folk. I suggest that we leave at once."

"Really?" I asked, cocking an eyebrow. "You don't want to remonstrate them for their poor taste?"

"Ah, no. No, I think not on the whole. No, I think we should leave, and not expose ourselves to this wretched place a second longer."

Not that I disagreed with him you understand, but I did rather enjoy to see him discomfited. I wanted to be out of that monster-haunted settlement as quick as possible!

"Well, I suppose so then," I conceded reluctantly. "I rather fancied stopping somewhere for a bite to eat."

"No! No," he continued more calmly, "We must press on. We'll never reach Canterbury at this rate, and B. will be quite as fat, if not fatter by the time we get there, if we stop for a square meal every half hour. No, we must press on!" With that he lowered his head and marched double-time straight through the village. I shared an amused glance with B., which was cut short by a loud roar from not so very far off. We hurried after the retreating figure of G.

Chapter 10

*How morality is multi-layered and not at
all straight forward. How Christians are
expected to do better.*

We walked on for two hours without much talk. Indeed, the impressive and sustained turn of speed that G. had put on meant that I hadn't any breath spare for chatting, while poor B. was soon puffing and gasping like an old bellows.

"I say G, hold up!" I called after him. "If we go like this any longer, B.'s going to burst something, and I'm the one likely to get caught in the blast! I really don't fancy having half of even such a close friend as B. splattered all over me."

G. turned and stared past me into the distance, back the way we had come. He eventually seemed satisfied and nodded. "Okay then. We'll have a rest."

B. collapsed onto the verge so heavily that via a complex application of chaos theory within the earth's crust, he caused a minor earthquake in California. We only discovered this later of course, and there is no conclusive proof that it was B's fault. He has refused to send the Californian government financial compensation and the case continues to drag through the international courts.

I got out the map and studied it. I figured out where we

were, circled the village we had passed and annotated it 'Here be dinosaurs!' G. noticed, and I expected some kind of withering remark, but he merely glanced over his shoulder and shook his head slightly.

In improving the map's accuracy however, I noticed my favourite cartographical symbol. The one that denotes 'Here be a public house'.

"I say you fellows, there's a pub in the vicinity!"

B. peered over my shoulder. "Are you sure?"

"Of course I'm sure! Look!" I stabbed at the page with my finger.

"And it definitely exists does it?" B. wondered.

"There's only one way to find out!" I declared, jumping up. I felt newly invigorated, and the rapidity with which B. heaved himself upright implied that he too felt the same boost of energy and spirits. When a tired man discovers that he is in the same district as a 'Here be a pub' sign, all his cares and weariness shed away, and he finds that he has another half a mile or more in him that had previously gone unrecognised.

G. quickly realised that this would enable us to keep moving, and so he enthusiastically agreed. We marched on, bright-eyed and bushy-whiskered, heads up and eyes straining for the first sign of a hospitable house.

We eventually rounded a corner, and saw it, much to my relief. It was a little further than I had expected, and I was beginning to worry that it really was one of the cartographical lies that we had discussed earlier.

We entered to find a pleasant little country pub of the best possible type. We ordered our drinks (I elected to go for a good dark porter of a kind happily becoming more common again) and seated ourselves in soft, leather-backed chairs that we sank down into to a surprising but entirely pleasant depth.

Having had a few sips of my beer, which was excellent, and cast an eye over the lunch menu, I found myself rather in need, if you catch my drift. Hearing the call of the wild. I excused myself and located the lavatories.

I found a cubicle and sat myself down in it. I was just gathering my resources and was about to get down to business, when glancing at the floor, I saw something lying there.

Bending forwards, I picked it up. It was a roll of bank notes, mostly twenties I believe, all held together by one of those metal clip devices. What some people find wrong with a good old-fashioned wallet is quite beyond me but there you go. Either way, I was holding in my hand what I estimated to be a cool two or three hundred pounds. Not small change by anyone's measure!

Well, I can honestly say that the idea of actually keeping it never occurred to me. It glimmered up in my brain as an available option, but not once did I even consider it. I hadn't noticed anyone else in the pub, so I determined to hand it over to the landlord.

This decision made I went back to the business of doing that which cannot be done for you by another, no matter how well you know them. Suddenly there was a knock on the cubicle door.

"Um, hello?" a hesitant voice said.

"Ah, good afternoon." I ventured. Toilet conversation is not something that Englishmen excel at. In fact, I am a strong supporter of the movement to make it completely illegal. Very trying business, but this chap was having none of it.

"Um, I don't suppose you found anything in there did you?"

"Oh, no, not at all," I reassured him. "It was all flushed

away when I got here."

"No, I mean in the cubicle. On the floor perhaps. I've lost some money and I thought that perhaps it had fallen out of my pocket while I was in there."

"Aha! Does it look anything like this?" I asked, pushing the bundle under the door.

"That's it!" he exclaimed, relief flooding his voice. "Thank you!"

"Not at all. Glad I could help."

"Oh, thank you so much! You've just saved my life!"

I began to wonder if he was a spy, or possibly a gangster. "Oh, no, really, not a problem."

I heard hurried footsteps as he exited the privy. I nodded to myself, satisfied that I had done my duty.

As I pulled up my trousers, it suddenly dawned on me how completely automatic my response had been to the situation. Not for a moment had I considered keeping the money for myself.

I smiled. What a good man I was! What a thoroughly and utterly decent fellow. Practically drowning in the milk of human kindness and stuffed with the cheese of charity; a soul lubricated with the butter of altruism and doused in the low-fat organic yoghurt of honour.

I exited that lavatory warmed and enchanted with my own purity, and sat back down with my travelling companions quite satisfied in and with myself.

"I say you chaps," I said, adopting an air of wry irritation. "I've just done myself out of three hundred quid!"

"Oh?" said B. "Well that was silly of you."

"How'd you manage that," G. asked.

"Ah, well a fellow had dropped a wad of cash on the toilet floor, but he came back for it. Of course I could have pretended not to have seen it, but that's not my way."

They nodded appreciatively. "Very decent of you," B. acknowledged.

"Why yes," said I, in a tone of mild surprise. "I suppose it was really, wasn't it?"

I drank my beer slowly, basking in my own goodness. I wondered whether or not I could cry off this silly pilgrimage business now. It had obviously done me a world of good, and had taken with me far faster than with my friends. I couldn't see that I really needed to walk all the way to Canterbury, although we were getting pretty close now. Why, that silly leaflet of sins was all gross exaggeration surely? I will admit that I needed a bit of a moral top-up, but now I was cured and in the pink of spiritual health.

I had successfully avoided greed, envy, sloth (impossible to sleep in a cold tent with Montgomery gnawing at your toe!) and all the rest.

And then my heart sank. Oh. The one sin I had been free of before, that is to say pride, seemed to have sidled in while I was sweeping out the rest of them; caught me in the flank as it were. A devilish and sneaky way to do things! Cowardly I call it!

I slumped in my chair. B. noticed. G. didn't. Selfish prig is G., uncaring of the state of his fellow man. Rotter!

"You're looking a little peaky there, J.," B. said. He didn't actually sound very concerned, but at least he paid lip-service to brotherly love. G. glanced over and raised an eyebrow.

"This is all really very hard," I said heavily.

"What's that then? I thought the beer was none too bad at all."

"Not the beer. Morality."

G. nodded at this. "Yes, tricky stuff that. Slippery."

"No, I wouldn't call it slippery," I said. "It's more like an onion."

B. looked puzzled at this. "It makes you cry?"

"No, it tastes vile, it smells worse and it has a great many layers, each one more eye-wateringly disgusting than the last."

They both nodded. My dislike for the common onion is well known amongst my peers and they accepted it without comment.

"That money," I said, "seemed very much to me like a test."

G. instantly looked sceptical. "Don't go ascribing purpose to random events now, J. That way lies madness."

"Well it seems to me that simply giving the money back wasn't the test at all. It was expected that I should do it automatically! The same way someone in an exam doesn't get marks simply for being able to hold a pen. If I couldn't hold a pen then obviously I would have failed from the start."

"Well yes. Is this going to be about your nosebleed again?"

"Hang my nosebleeds! Let's assume that I'm not talking about a physics paper! The real test was after the event. Okay, I gave that blasted fellow his money back. But that shouldn't have even been an issue. The way I see, there were two further layers of this vile onion of morality. One was telling you chaps about it, and the other was being proud of myself for doing something which should have been automatic in the first place."

"Ah," G. nodded. "You think you should have been good simply as a matter of course, not as a matter of note?"

"Precisely. But then it gets worse. If I hadn't told you two about it then I would still have had to avoid sitting here being proud at myself!"

"Why?"

"Pardon?"

"What's wrong with being proud of yourself for being good? Lots of people aren't you know."

"Well..." I paused, stumped for a moment. "There shouldn't be anything to be proud of, should there? It shouldn't register as 'good'. It shouldn't register at all. It's just something that should happen."

"That seems awfully harsh," B. opined. "Surely all the reward of being good is to feel proud and have people know what a thoroughly decent chap you are?"

"It seems like there might be better rewards for keeping it quiet and not making a braggart of yourself though."

"Hmph! I am unconvinced by that."

"But if you do it for praise, you're not doing it to be good. Your motive is that much less pure."

"But if you're doing it in hope of pie in the sky, how is that any purer?"

"You shouldn't be doing it for air-born pies either though, or any other delicious sky-bound snack. To say that good is its own reward is, to my mind at least, a gross over-simplification. You shouldn't do a good deed for the reward of having done it; you should do it for no other reason than it is *right* that it be done."

"So you shouldn't do good deeds for the reward of eternal life?" G. asked frowning.

"I don't think so, no," I said after a few moments' thought. "I suppose that getting an afterlife should be seen as a much-appreciated bonus, but certainly not the aim. I think that in this case, the means is far more important than the ends. In fact, I reckon that if the means are done right, and for the right reasons, then the ends will take care of themselves, whatever they might be. Or perhaps I should say that the ends will be taken care of for us."

G. raised an eyebrow at this. "That," he said firmly, "remains to be seen."

I paused, and nodded. We finished our meals in silence.

Chapter 11

The case against the biblical view of homosexuality and the doctrine of Hell.

After lunch, we continued on our way, my brain still reeling from the multi-layered net of writhing moral spaghetti within which I had found myself to be an unsuspecting meatball.

The day had become overcast, and the three of us slogged on in silence. Eventually we came upon a small town, the name of which I shall neglect to repeat for reasons that shall soon become apparent. The odds are that you heard about it on the news in any case, so it might well be superfluous.

As we entered the town, B. started to speculate about whether or not there was a decent pub hereabouts.

"Look here," I said sharply, "we seem to have spent half our time in pubs! If we hadn't stopped at quite so many, we might well have been there and on the way back by now."

"But all of this walking makes me hungry and thirsty. Besides, you've not been complaining before. You've just sat there and guzzled with G. and me. In fact, the last one was your idea!"

"That was entirely necessary," I replied with some considerable dignity. "It was also not so very long ago."

"And I do not guzzle," G. said firmly. "I eat and drink

with precision and dignity."

"Yes, you're thinking of Monty," I cut in snidely.

"Monty eats with dignity as well! J. wouldn't recognise it of course. He has all the dignity of a one-legged hippo."

Before I could come back with my own piercing riposte, we were all shocked by a series of yells and cries. We instinctively ducked and I looked around wildly for the dinosaur. None was forthcoming, but the shouting continued from around the next corner.

Cautiously, we approached the turning. Even the usually blasé Monty was staying close to G.'s ankles, although this might well have simply been to trip him.

Peering carefully around it, we saw a large crowd of people gathered around outside what I took to be a magistrate's court. They seemed extremely worked up about something, and I could see a television crew filming it all. Since there didn't seem to be any prehistoric behemoths rampaging about the place, we decided that it would be safe to approach.

We moved towards the crowd. Some of them were holding up placards, but since they were facing the courthouse, we couldn't read any of them. I stepped up to one of the rear-most protesters, a serious-looking chap in his late middle-age.

"I say, what's all this about then?"

He turned with an expression of surprise on his face, but this quickly hardened into set-jawed determination. "We are here sir," he said firmly, "to ensure that our children are protected from the worst and most perverse forms of human behaviour."

"Oh." I nodded, impressed. "Good stuff that. Protecting your children, not perverse behaviour that is," I added hurriedly. This looked like the sort of crowd to jump to conclusions. A bit lynch-mobbish around the edges if you catch my meaning.

"So, um, not that I want to pry too far into the perversities, but what exactly is going on?"

"We are here to ensure that our local by-laws are maintained. There's a 'trial' going on in there. Sort of a test case. The wishy-washy liberal establishment are trying to overturn our ancient and dearly held traditions, and we won't have it!"

I nodded sagely at this little tirade and mentally pigeon-holed him under 'Daily Express Reader'. "All very bad and not at all sporting I'm sure, but what is it that these beasts in human form, these gross and gratuitous barbarians, these sink-holes of human depravity, have actually done?"

He glared at me, no doubt trying to figure out if I was being sarcastic. For the record, I wasn't, although I concede that I may perhaps have been laying it on a bit thick.

"They... they sleep with their feet by the headboard." He curled his lips as he said it, as though the very words left a foul taste in his mouth.

"Ah. That's... not really so very bad is it?"

He stared at me open-mouthed. If I'd suggested we strip naked and start wrestling one another in a bath of Marmite, he could not have been more shocked and disgusted.

"Not bad? NOT BAD? Why do you think it's called a headboard!?"

"Well, obviously one is supposed to sleep with the head by it, or possibly because it's at the head of the bed. I've never really thought about it to be honest." I paused, lost in contemplation of the question for a moment, before wrenching my attention back to the disgruntled chap before me. "Sorry, yes, um, is it really so very bad to sleep with your feet by it?"

"Certainly it is! Why, someone who sleeps with his feet by the headboard might do anything! If we allow that then what next? Nude parades down our high streets? Reading from the Kama Sutra for the under-fives? Mobility scooters for the able-bodied?"

"Um, actually I don't think you have to be disabled to..."

"No sir, we will not stand for it! We will not allow the rot to set in! We will not allow the thin end of the wedge to hold open the door that leads into the corridor of filth!"

"Ah... Right ho then." I was on the verge of giving in and moving away in case it was contagious, but I decided to give it another go. I had had time to inspect the crowd, and they were all of an age with the fellow I was addressing. None of them looked up to a sustained turn of speed, and I reckoned I might be able to get away if they came over all torches-and-pitchforks. "But look here, surely it doesn't matter what a person does in the bedroom does it?"

"Certainly it does! Sleeping with your feet by the headboard is deeply immoral!"

"But why is it immoral?"

"Because it's against our by-laws, and they wouldn't have put it in if it wasn't immoral would they?"

"But why is it immoral? What's immoral about it?"

He looked blank. I had clearly gone beyond him. "Look, if I kill a fellow, or go out and steal a chap's bicycle, I have clearly committed an immoral act, because I've hurt or deprived someone else."

He nodded. This was obviously the sort of stuff he could grasp.

"But if I sleep with my feet by the headboard, at the very

worst my toe-nails might scratch the varnish, and since it's my own bed, that's my own problem. How I go about positioning myself in my bed is surely my own affair, as long as no one else is hurt by it, yes?"

"But it's specifically prohibited as an immoral abomination in the by-laws!"

"Then change the by-law!"

His jaw dropped. His eyes goggled. His cheeks drained of colour and I was afraid he was about to have a conniptic fit of some kind. "You can't do that! You can't just go round changing the law! You can't go cherry-picking the laws you like and ignoring the ones you don't!"

"I don't see why not!" I will admit that I was getting rather heated now. There is nothing that frustrates me more than blunt ignorance, and my blood was well and truly up. "If you look at the law, and it says don't kill, or don't steal, or don't commit fraud or speed or take things that will mess up your brain and then kill you, all of which make sense, and then it suddenly says something stupid like 'Persons sleeping the wrong way up in bed will be imprisoned', it seems fairly obvious that one is an odd one out. It doesn't fit with any of the other laws; it's outlawing something pretty much utterly harmless and is quite frankly probably a clerical error or a practical joke by a bored secretary!"

He shook his head and smiled a smug little smile. "You obviously don't understand the seriousness of the matter sirs."

The plural caught me off-guard, and I turned to see that G. and B. had followed me. I had been too worked up to notice them.

"No sirs, the punishment for foot-boarding is not imprisonment at all."

"A small fine then is it? An Anti-Social Sleeping

Behaviour Order?" G. inquired with a cool politeness.

"Oh no. They are tortured most severely, and then eventually killed. All at the state's expense."

"Egad!" I exclaimed. "For sleeping upside down in bed?"

He nodded. "The wretches deserve nothing better!"

B. scratched his head. "I thought that the death penalty had been repealed, except in cases of repeated talking during films, plays and operas?"

"Ah, that's the joy of living in this borough," the man replied with a smile. "Our ancient by-laws still stand unaffected. An Act of Parliament enacted in 1894 protects them in perpetuity."

"So if that's the punishment for sleeping upside down, what's the punishment for theft?"

"Prolonged torture, followed by a painful death."

"Crikey! And murder?"

"Prolonged torture, followed by a painful death."

G. nodded. "Ah, a pattern emerges. And for rape?"

"Extended torture, horrible messy demise sir."

"Right. Video piracy? Vandalism? Public indecency? Drunk and disorderly?"

"Torture sir, for as lengthy a period as the perpetrator can stand, followed by an excruciatingly slow and painful death."

"What about allowing a dog to foul on public property?" I asked innocently. "Or allowing said animal to steal? Say, for example, beer or a bra?"

"The animal would be tortured and killed in front of its owner, and then the owner would be tortured and killed."

"Really?" I glanced sidelong at G., who had scooped Monty up in his arms and was glaring viciously at me.

"And what," said he pointedly, "would be the punishment for slanderous talk about a perfectly respectable and very well-trained dog?"

The man nodded. "Ah, good question. Depending on circumstances and having ascertained that the talk was indeed slanderous, the culprit would be tortured and then killed."

I scratched my head and pondered on this for a few moments. I was pretty sure that there wasn't a court in the land who'd convict me if only I was allowed to use Monty as evidence, but I didn't fancy risking it. "You don't perhaps think that the punishment is somewhat out of proportion to the crimes? I mean, there might be an argument for murder or rape, although I don't see it myself, but being tortured to death for video piracy?"

"It's in the by-laws sir, and they wouldn't have made them like that if it weren't for a good reason!"

"But torture and killing are against the law!"

"Oh yes sir, very much so, and punishable by torture and death."

"But the by-laws see fit to expose people to the self-same treatment that it specifically condemns?"

"It's not for us to question the by-laws sir. They knew what they were doing when they put that book together."

"It seems to me, "I said, "that there is a very good case for going through your by-laws and having a good think about some of the stuff in there. It seems that some of it is completely out of keeping with the general character, and should possibly be moved to the appendices."

"That's what the Marxists in London want sir! And that's why we're protesting!"

It was at this point that we realised that we had been overheard by several other protesters, and some of them were holding their placards in a very menacing fashion. I suddenly didn't feel as swift as I had a few moments before.

"Well, good luck with your protest," I said, smiling weakly. "We need to go now."

We proceeded to beat a hasty retreat, walked quickly through the town and left as quickly as possible. If you didn't see the news coverage, you will be glad to hear that the borough by-laws of _____ were over-turned, and the county torture-chamber and execution rooms were turned first into a lunatic asylum, then a school for seriously disturbed psychics before finally being rented out to small groups of over-daring teenagers and cocky paranormal research teams, many of whom were never seen again.

Chapter 12

***The pure reason for doing good is that we
have already been rewarded in full. Or on
how Christianity is all back to front.***

Another hour or so of walking brought us into the vicinity of
a particularly picturesque little place, all hanging baskets and
wooded roads and tidy little houses with well-kept front
gardens. One of those little villages that's strung out along a
road with fifty yards between each house, a maximum total
width of about forty yards and a total length of about a mile.
An utterly charming spot. The village sported a B&B of
which I had read much to the good, and we had determined to
make this our destination for the day.

However, due to the enforced haste with which we had
exited from the previous two settlements, we were rather
ahead of our timetable, and had an hour or so to kill before
dinner, so we determined to walk into the middle (perhaps I
should say mid-point) of the village. It had become an
extremely pleasant day, the late afternoon sun coming down
mellow and warming. Between the houses we could see green
fields and verdant trees, and we were in a state of
considerable contentment.

We suddenly heard a high-pitched ringing noise behind

us, and turning we saw a little old lady wobbling towards us on a bicycle of considerable vintage. She pulled up next to us with a quiet squeal of un-oiled brakes and smiled benevolently at us.

"Pardon me my dears, but could you give me some numbers please?"

We looked at her blankly, but she smiled again. "Any numbers dears, between nought and one hundred. Different ones each if you'd be so kind."

We glanced at each other, somewhat bemused, but she seemed such a sweet old thing, and the request seemed so harmless that we really couldn't find it in ourselves to refuse her. I suggested thirty-six, which is a favourite number of mine, G. proffered seventy-five, while B. contributed forty-seven. The lady pulled a stub of pencil out of her hat and a crumpled piece of paper from a pocket and scribbled them down.

"Fantastic! Thank you so much! Only three more to get today. Good afternoon."

We nodded and smiled to her, and she pushed off and started pedalling down the road. We looked at each other once more, still utterly bemused, and not a little entertained. We continued walking for another fifteen minutes, before turning around and heading back to our hostelry.

Dinner, when it was served was fantastic, and we offered our hosts numerous compliments. The elderly couple who ran the bed and breakfast were kindly and polite, and their house was clean, neat and comfortable.

As the lady began to clear away our plates, G. glanced up at her. "Pardon me."

She beamed at him. "Yes?"

"We were approached by a lady as we walked into the

village. She wanted us to give her some random numbers."

Understanding dawned on the good woman's face and she nodded. "Oh yes. That'll be Elsa."

"Ah. What does she need them for? The numbers I mean."

"Oh, well it's a bit of a strange story truth to tell. A bit of a local curiosity you might say."

"We certainly might, if we were to be told a little more about it."

"Ah, well you see Elsa was asking for lottery numbers. You see, she is playing the Reverse Lottery." She beamed at us, happy in the knowledge that she had cleared up the confusion.

We looked at each other. "And what," I asked politely, "might the Reverse Lottery be? If you get the right numbers does a big company come and take away several million pounds of your money? What do they do if you don't have as much as they want?"

"Oh no! Nothing like that! No, it's all the idea of a local billionaire. He must be a very eccentric sort of man. Generous to a fault though."

"I take it you've not met him then?"

She shook her head. "No one has. Well, except Elsa. He has agreed to give her fifty million pounds."

"What, for nothing!" B. exclaimed. He is very much a capitalist, and these sorts of goings on cut him to the core.

"We're not sure. One of the stipulations of the deal, as Elsa explains it anyway, is that now she's won the prize, he wants her to get the right numbers."

"And how will she know when she gets them?"

"She posts the ticket to him each week."

G. frowned at this. "But if she's already got the money, then why is she bothering to try and find the numbers? It makes a mockery of logic! How can anyone possibly say 'Here is the prize, you can have it now. Afterwards you can try and win it.' Or is that a stipulation of the transaction? Is the prize dependent on her continued attempts to win it?" Trust G. to use a phrase like 'stipulation of the transaction'. And to an old lady too!

"We really don't know, sir. You're not the first one to have asked that, and Elsa herself is a little confused about it. In fact there's been an awful lot of argument about the whole thing. She's been to see solicitors, but they tell her different things. She went into London to the offices of Wesley, Wesley and Whitfield, and Mr Wesley … I'm not sure which one … told her that she did indeed have to keep trying to get the numbers. He said that the deal would be null and void otherwise."

"I see. Well that sounds quite fair," B. said. "And it's not really so much to ask is it, in exchange for several million of quid."

"Ah, but on the way out Mr Whitfield said that his colleague might well be wrong, and that she should go and talk to the firm of Calvin, Bunyan and Knox and get a second opinion. Well she did that, and having heard her story, they said that the deal was concluded, and that now the money was in her possession, her benefactor couldn't legally demand it back. However, they did advise her to keep on getting the numbers, if only as a sign of good faith."

G. nodded. "I take it she didn't get a paper contract out of this fellow? The billionaire I mean."

She shook her head. "Oh no, it was all done quite informally I believe. Anyway, she decided to get a third opinion, and went to Agricola, Amsdorf and Vane. They confirmed Mr Calvin's opinion, but said that there was absolutely no requirement for her to continue trying to get the winning numbers."

We all nodded. "So what did she decide to do?" I asked.

"Ah, well she decided to play it safe you see, and carry on getting the numbers. She said that Wesley, Wesley and Whitfield's answer seemed fairest to her, and as you say it's not that much to do is it? Not compared to what he's done for her anyway. She was living in abject poverty before, and he's gone and lifted her up and turned her life around."

"I should say it's not much!" B. said. "Unbelievable generosity! As you say, the old fish must be quite barmy."

We nodded our agreement. "Absolutely crackers," I concurred. "Where can we find him? I don't suppose he's dishing out any more free fortunes is he?"

"Not so far as I know, but then I'm not sure anyone's asked. He's away at the moment anyway."

"Shame, I'd very much like to have met him."

G. shrugged. "I'm not so sure. Don't get me wrong, a few million pounds would be handy, but having to fill in a load of lottery tickets every week would be a bit of a bind to be honest."

"She certainly wasn't forced into the deal, sir," our hostess said. "She was given every opportunity to refuse it, but she thought it seemed worth it, and in her place I'm sure I'd do the same. If I meet the gentleman, I'll certainly accept!"

"Unfortunately that seems as unlikely for you as it does for us. We're moving on tomorrow so it's odds on that we'll miss him." I sighed.

"You might yet see him, sir. They say he's got a big old house in Canterbury somewhere, if you ever find yourselves in the area."

The three of us looked at each other and grinned. It seemed that there might be hope for us yet!

Chapter 13

The nature of Christ. How unlikely is something that has happened, and will only happen, once?

We slept very well that night, in large, clean and comfortable beds. It knocked tents and sleeping bags into an old hat and no mistake! Breakfast was as sumptuous and capacious as dinner had been, and our hosts just as kindly and polite. We took our leave of them with no little regret, but set our feet towards our ever-nearing destination and marched off.

The sun was shining, the birds were singing and all of nature seemed present, correct and in tip-top condition. Walking through that little village was a pleasure, fresh as we were from our beds, and with breakfast still warming our stomachs.

To the right of the road, amongst some trees, we saw a placid pond. Beside it sat a young girl, apparently alone. She looked up as we drew near and considered us solemnly.

"Excuse me," she said.

We beamed at her benevolently. "Yes my dear?" I said cheerfully. "Although you really shouldn't talk to strangers you know."

She frowned and appeared to think about this for a few

seconds, then seemed to decide that since she'd already broken this rule she may as well tell us what she wanted anyway.

"Do you know anything about frogs?"

The three of us looked at each other, and even Monty pricked up an ear. His frog-battling exploits were legendary in certain quarters. Quarters which queued up at G.'s door demanding redress for terrified fish, torn pond-liners and trails of mud and pondweed across their previously pristine lawns. I glared at him, and G. shortened his lead.

I turned back to the girl. "Oh yes! We are very knowledgeable on the subject of frogs. What is it about frogs that you wished to know?"

She frowned again. "Can they be princes sometimes?"

We paused, momentarily taken aback. We then glanced at each other, smiling quietly. I nodded sagely. "You've heard the story of the Frog Prince?"

"My mum read it to me last night, but I don't think it was real. I've been looking at the frogs in the pond, and I don't think any of them are princes."

"Princes are a little thin on the ground," G. agreed. "More republics around nowadays."

"But princes are tall. How could a big tall handsome prince with a crown and a sword get squished down into a little frog?"

"Oh, well it was magic wasn't it?"

This did not appear to satisfy her.

"That doesn't explain anything! I don't think he was a prince at all!" She paused after this little outburst and thought for a couple of seconds, pouting. "He was probably a very nice frog," she conceded. "He was probably very charming, sort of like a prince would be, but he was only a frog really."

"But why do you say that?" B. asked her kindly. "That sort of thing happened more back then. Not nowadays of course. We don't really have magic anymore."

"It doesn't seem very likely." A precocious girl this!

"But not very likely compared to what?" I asked. "It only ever happened once, so you can't really say that it's likely or unlikely. After all, you've only ever been born once in the history of the world. Does that mean that you don't exist?"

"No, I'm real!" She seemed really quite indignant that I might think anything else.

"But you existing at all is surely only as likely as the prince being turned into a frog isn't it?"

She considered this. Monty had trundled up to her and she was now scratching his head and stroking him as she pondered. "Maybe... I think he was probably lying about being a prince."

"What, so he could go home with the princess and sleep in a nice warm bed instead of a cold wet pond?"

"Yes, but that would mean he was liar, and not very nice. Mummy says lying is very naughty."

"Your mother is a wise lady. You tell the truth young woman, and you'll always come right."

"Perhaps he was just mistaken. Maybe he thought that he was a prince, but really he was only a frog all along."

We all thought about this. "You mean he was a frog who honestly thought he was a prince?" B. said hesitantly. "A frog with delusions of grandeur?"

She pouted. "I don't know what that means! I think he was crazy!"

"But the point still stands," I pointed out, "that he claimed to be a prince. So you have to decide whether you think he was lying, crazy or royal. Perjurer, pea-brain or prince?"

She nodded, deep in thought.

"Besides, haven't you heard the end of the story?" I asked.

"No. I fell asleep before mummy got to the end."

"Ah, well you ask her for the end tonight, and you'll see how it turned out," I advised. "Now we really must be going. It was very nice to have met you."

She smiled at us, and we turned and marched on up the road, leaving her staring thoughtfully down into the water.

Chapter 14

On the existence of moral atheists. Why they can exist, but could do better.

The weather being as fine as it was, our progress was excellent that morning, and by eleven o'clock the road was passing between grassy fields with only the occasional distant spire to mark where the village lay.

Suddenly the hedgerow to our left came to a stop, to be replaced instead with a simple wooden fence. On the other side we could see a large green field. In the field were a large number of horses. Some of them had riders, others hadn't, and they all seemed to be milling around. Several other men were standing around apparently trying to enforce some sort of order to the proceedings.

We decided to take a break, and leant against the fence to watch. At some unseen signal, about a third of the horses, all ones with riders, suddenly made a rush for the far end of the field, galloping as swiftly as they could. Some of the riderless horses followed, although rather more slowly. Other horses with riders remained where they were, and though the riders watched their companions race, they seemed to make no effort to persuade their steeds to follow. Quite a few of the riderless horses, along with the horses of the listless jockeys, evidently excited by all the commotion also started galloping, but in whichever direction they happened to be facing at the time, so that there was a sudden equine diaspora, exploding outward across the field.

Having reached the far end of the field, the riders turned their mounts back and trotted back to where they had started. Other men hurried over to bring the riderless horses back to the start, and it appeared that they would soon repeat the process.

Monty had been quite interested in all of this running up and down and galloping about, and now he loudly voiced his admiration and encouragement, with much jumping up and down and wagging of his hindquarters.

We saw two men detach themselves from the crowd of horses and riders and start ambling over to us. We waited as they approached. Both were middle-aged men of prosperous appearance. They smiled as they drew closer.

"Good day to you sirs," one of them said with a tip of his hat.

The three of us nodded back. "And a good day to you too," I replied amiably.

"So you're watching our tests are you?" the gentleman asked, smiling.

"Is that what they are?" B. asked.

"Yes, they are. The future of horse-racing lies here in this very field."

We looked at him with surprise.

"Oh?" said B. B. has been known to enjoy a flutter or two every Friday or so, and any development in the sport was naturally of great interest to him.

"Yes indeed," said the other man, "and that being so could we please ask you to keep your dog quiet? We are trying to be as scientifically rigorous as possible and we don't want any loud noises startling the animals."

G. picked Monty up in his arms. "Of course. I do apologise. He just got a little over excited by all the action. He's really very interested in science."

I choked loudly and started coughing. G, glared at me with all the lethal power that he could bestow. "Yes?"

"Oh, nothing," I spluttered. "Swallowed a fly or some-such I imagine."

G. grunted and turned back to the two men. "So what are you trying to do here? If it's not a secret that is."

The two men glanced at each other for a second. The one on the left nodded, and his colleague turned back to us. "My friend and I have been having something of a dispute, and these experiments are our attempt to settle it."

His companion nodded. "You see, it is my belief that a horse, being a natural runner, evolved over millennia to move rapidly across grasslands, does not actually need a jockey to encourage them. Indeed, a horse without jockey, saddle or any of the other tack should be able to run faster than a horse which is weighed down by all the apparatus."

"Of course, I disagree," his friend said. "While I am perfectly happy to admit that a riderless horse is just as capable of running and winning a race as a horse with a jockey, why should a horse gallop itself to exhaustion if it has no direction in which to gallop? A horse unweighted by rider and harness might well run faster, but it is highly unlikely that it will run in the correct direction. Imagine a derby in which every horse runs in it whichever way it pleased! You'd have no idea who'd won!"

"Horses like to gallop!" his friend interjected impatiently. I had the distinct impression that this argument had been replayed numerous times between the two men. "They are naturally running animals and have absolutely no need of direction or steering of any sort to run. They are herd animals and will all run in the same direction."

"But what if that one direction is wrong? And why should they run? What motivates them to do so?"

"A simple love of running, the natural-born instinct to gallop as fast as they can, to gallop with the herd!"

"I contend that that is insufficient!"

They glared at each other for a second, before both sighing. The fellow on the right, the jockey-less advocate, smiled. "You see gentlemen? That is why we are running these tests. There are thirty horses in this field. Ten of them have riders and tack as normal. Ten have riders, but only have saddles. The other ten have neither riders nor tack of any description."

We nodded. "I see," G. said. "So the horses with riders but no tack are a control group?"

The fellow nodded enthusiastically. "Indeed. On a given signal, the ten riders with reins and spurs turn their horses towards the opposite end of the field and ride as fast as they can. The ten without reins and spurs simply sit in the saddles and allow the horses to do as they wish. The horses without riders are also allowed to do as they wish."

We nodded. "I see," I said, "and what have your findings been so far?"

"It's very early in the experiment to be sure. We intend to run the horses a great many times. The more testing we do, the greater the degree of accuracy we can arrive at. However I might venture to say at this point that the riderless horses very much lack direction, and only a few of them bother running after the horses that are steered and spurred on. Even these tend to lag behind and not take the lead."

"We can't know that!" his friend interrupted. "We must refuse to make any speculations until we can review the results fully. I maintain that here today we are going to revolutionise racing forever, and do away with the silly and inhumane use of reins!"

The two set to arguing loudly again, so we simply said our goodbyes and continued along the road, enjoying the sunshine. Behind us, over the sound of arguing, came the thundering rumble of the horses galloping across the field.

Chapter 15

Denying something because you've never experienced it yourself is small-mindedness of the worst kind.

We had not gone very much further before we found ourselves in a smallish town, or perhaps a largish village. The sun continued to beat down on us, and we had all returned to that blissful state of mind where one can sit back, so to speak, and simply enjoy being alive.

We ambled contentedly along the street, basking in the sunlight and breathing in the clean, balmy air. Wispish clouds floated lazily overhead, drifting amidst the bright blue of the ether. Birds sang, bees buzzed about and all seemed right with the world.

A chap with a dog approached us along the road and, as he got closer, we noticed that he held a white cane in his hand.

Monty eyed the approaching hound with suspicion. It was an Alsatian, and therefore several times the size of Monty. Issues of scale, however, have never intruded into either Monty's pugnaciousness or his lust, and so he advanced, determined to discover which of these he should unleash upon the approaching giant. However, the guide-dog was far too well brought up to do likewise, which I pointed out with some relish to G.

"He's not being rude," G. pointed out peevishly. "He's being friendly. He's just saying hello."

"That's one way of looking at it," I conceded.

Having got into close proximity with the stranger, the difference in respective altitudes seemed to dawn on Monty. He looked the beast up and down, then up some more to take it all in, then appeared to reach a decision and sauntered nonchalantly, but perhaps a little too quickly back to G., where he took up a relaxed position behind his leg.

"Good day to you," I said, to the behemoth's owner cheerily.

The man looked in our direction and nodded. "I suppose so. The air's very warm, and there's not much wind."

"Indeed not. The sun's shining and there's hardly a cloud in the sky," I replied, perhaps in retrospect a little insensitively, but with no intended malice.

He sneered. "Oh please!" he said contemptuously. "Don't play the fool with me. It's no good you know. I'm blind, not stupid!"

This took my companions and I rather aback. I replayed my words back to myself, and acknowledged that perhaps they had been poorly chosen, but failed to see how they could imply that the fellow was lacking in the cranial department.

"Um... Pardon?"

He curled his lip. "Do you really hope to take me in with that sun, sky and clouds malarkey?"

We looked at each other. G. frowned. "You're not related to Dick Dorking are you?"

"Certainly not! I've heard of him. The man's a nutcase! My name is Kit Kitchens."

"A self-made man are you?" B. asked. We looked at him.

91

"A self-made... his name's Kit Kitchens... a self...yes, well, I thought it was rather good."

There was an awkward pause. "Yes, well," G. said eventually, "you were saying about the clouds Mr Kitchens?"

"I wasn't saying anything about the clouds!" he snapped. "It would be pointless to do so since they patently do not exist."

"I'm very sorry, sir," G. replied, "but they do. I can assure you on that point."

"Nonsense! The very concept of clouds is ridiculous. Why, I see very little reason to believe that the earth's atmosphere is very much thicker than perhaps fifty or sixty feet."

"Ah, well, I can assure you again that you are in error, since I myself have been in buildings higher than that and I have not suffered any of the ill-effects of exposure to the cold hard vacuum of space."

"Hah! But since you're also the same crackpot who yammers on about clouds and the sun, I'm hardly likely to believe you when you say that now am I? You have lost all credibility."

This rather put G. aback. We looked at each other and scratched our heads.

"But what about the rain?" I asked. "How do you explain that, other than by clouds?"

He waved a hand dismissively. "If rain really fell from such a height as most cloud-believers claim, it would fall far harder than the gentle pattering which we experience. No, the rain falls from a mere ten or twenty feet above our heads."

"But that's simply not true!" G. exclaimed. "You're not taking into account air resistance, or terminal velocities or mass or anything like that! You're just dogmatically asserting!"

"And what are you doing then?" he riposted. "You've told yourselves the same precious lie so often that you've started to believe it! You've told yourselves about clouds and the sun and so on so often that now you actually see them wherever you look, even though there are perfectly rational explanations for what you're experiencing. It's only because I had the good fortune to be born blind that I haven't been taken in myself."

"So how do you explain the warmth of the sunlight?"

"Pah! Sun! There's no such thing. What I feel is merely the currents of air moving from warmer regions, thus heating me. And the wind itself cannot come from very far away. I know this because it changes direction so often, and would have to perform too wide a compass in order to do so."

"Yes," I began, "but…"

"And in case you were about to start on it, let's have no talk of moon or stars. What do they do? What are they for? They're even less convincing than the sun!"

"I'm sorry but you're quite wrong," said a voice. G. and I turned in surprise to find that it had come from B., and he had a most peculiar expression on his face.

"I beg your pardon?" our new acquaintance said, an expression of utmost shock on his face.

"I'm afraid that all of your arguments are of no avail, sir. You see, I have seen the black storms boil across the sky, swollen with wrath and thunder. I have watched the long grey rain fall on distant hills. I have gazed upon the gentle white clouds, roaming across the glorious blue sky in docile herds. I have seen the heavens torn apart by lightning, and I have seen them spread with stars, silent and vast and wonderful."

He paused, trying to gather more words, while G. and I

gaped at each other. He looked up again, the battle-light still shining in his eyes.

"You can use every trick of thought and language. You can appeal to logic and rationality, make point after solid point, and argument after endlessly clever argument until you're blue in the face and I don't know whether I'm coming or going. But it doesn't matter. It's all useless. It doesn't matter how clever you think you are; because I have seen the sky, and it is beautiful."

#

About ten minutes later, we left the town in silence. B. was stomping ahead with almost unheard of energy, leaving myself and G. to scuttle along in his wake.

"I say, B.! Hold up, there's a good fellow!" I cried out to him. He stopped and looked round at us as though surprised to see us there.

"Yes?"

"Where the devil did that come from?"

"Did what come from?"

G. and I looked at each other again, mouths open.

"Th-That!" G. yelped. "It... that was... My dear fellow!"

"I just didn't like to hear him talking like that about things he clearly doesn't understand."

"Yes, but what you said..."

He waved a hand in irritation. "Oh yes I'm sure it was stupid. 'Doltish old B. goes and puts his foot in it again.' I am not a clever man, so it irks me to hear those who suppose that they are clever quite clearly being completely back-headed about things and supposing that by doing so it shows them to be clever. Can we please not go on about it?"

"No! No, my good chap, it was... it was beautiful. It was incredible."

B. raised his eyebrows, but I nodded my agreement. "Dear fellow, it was poetry! It was magnificent! I do wonder though..."

"Yes?"

"Well, after your remarkable speech, do you really suppose you should have hit him like that, seeing as he was blind and all?"

Chapter 16

How religions cannot be held responsible for those that do not follow their commandments, even if they claim to be adherents.

We had walked for another twenty minutes or half an hour when we saw a woman coming towards us along the road. Nearing, we got the impression that she was a tramp of sorts, a lady traveller with no destination and no starting point, but a road beneath her feet and an itch in her soles that urged her out into the world.

She drew nearer and our initial appraisal was confirmed. Her clothes were grubby, her face was smudged with dirt and her shoes were falling to pieces before our eyes. It was the nature of said shoes and clothing though, that gave me pause for thought.

She was wearing what looked like it had once been a very smart business suit, and her shoes were of the absolute finest. She had a very battered, scuffed and positively disintegrating briefcase under one arm, and plastic shopping bags in each hand, filled with all sorts of bric-a-brac.

She smiled and nodded at us cheerfully. We smiled and nodded back and prepared to pass her when she cleared her throat. We looked at her.

"Excuse me gentlemen, but do any of you need a dietician?"

I tried not to glance at B. as I replied. "Ah, no thank you. We're absolutely fine in that regard, thank you."

"Or perhaps an animal behaviourist?"

This time I did glance very pointedly at Monty, who bared his teeth at me.

"It depends. Do you use electric-shock collars and choke-chains?"

"Oh no, certainly not!"

"Then no, thank you."

"How about a business strategy consultant?"

"No, I really don't think so. Sorry."

"Ah." She looked downcast and heaved a great sigh.

"If you don't mind me saying," G. began, "that's quite a repertoire you have there."

The lady nodded. "Oh yes. I'm very much a polymath. Or rather I was. No doubt you've heard of me. Martha Watkins is the name."

We looked at each other, but G. and I both drew a blank. B., however, frowned and scratched his head. "Watkins? As in the Watkins Diet?"

The ragged woman beamed. "That's me! Yes, I am the creator of the world-renowned Watkins Diet!"

I have to be honest, I'd never heard of it, but B. certainly seemed to know what he was talking about, having tried numerous diets in the past. I have to say though that despite being highly recommended by all sorts of extremely famous people, very few ever made more than a transitory impact on his waistline.

"What might the Watkins Diet consist of?" I asked. Gifted

from childhood with what I like to call a wiry frame, such things had never held much interest for me.

"Ah well," Miss Watkins began enthusiastically, "it consisted of a four-month course of eating reasonably-sized portions of healthy foods, three times a day, and taking at least an hour's good, or two hours' light, exercise each day. I could guarantee that within a couple of months weight loss would be markedly noticed."

"Well that sounds fairly straight forward. Why was it not a success?"

She ran a hand through her tangle of hair ruefully. "Well everyone who tried it started off well, eating healthily and exercising and so forth, but by the second week they were eating more and exercising less. By the third week they were eating as much, if not more, than before and not exercising at all. A group of them got together and sued me for causing them to gain weight."

"But surely that wasn't your fault?" G. asked. "If they weren't going to follow your instructions, they could hardly blame you."

"But they did! And popular opinion was on their side. It was well known that they were on my diet, and yet they gained weight. So I chucked in the dietician business and decided to become an animal behaviourist."

"That seems wise."

"Oh yes. I published 'The Watkins Dog Training Guide', to great critical acclaim."

"Not great enough," I murmured, glancing at Monty. Monty cocked his head and looked at me curiously. I gave him a tight smile and turned back to our new acquaintance.

"In it, I recommended a system of firm but gentle discipline with a dog. The owner was instructed to use treats and positive reinforcement just as much, if not considerably more than punishments and negative reinforcement. I specifically prohibited any sort of genuine violence towards the animal."

"Ah, you see, you really should have stuck to dieticianing," I said, shaking my head. "You clearly do not understand animals. Or at any rate have never met Monty. He would reverse your opinions on violence towards animals in a flash."

If looks could kill, I would have been at the centre of a G.-induced thermo-nuclear detonation.

"Ignore my ignorant and sadistic companion," said he. "He does not understand animals. They are too intelligent for him, and make him feel quite inadequate."

"But at least I don't lead a mangy baby substitute round on a lead!"

"Not at all! No doubt you'll do that to your actual baby if the world is ever so unfortunate as to see a continuation of your line!"

"I…" I was interrupted by B. clearing his throat noisily.

"You were saying Miss Watkins?"

She, taken aback (by G.'s rudeness no doubt) took a few seconds to collect herself. "Ah, yes. Well having given this advice about rewards and treats and no violence and whatnot, I got lots of business. Life was good for a while. I wrote a book based on the Watkins Dog Training Method, and it sold fairly well."

We all nodded. A woman enjoying the fruits of her labours. All good and proper and showing the march of capitalism in all of its glory.

She saw our expressions and smiled sadly. "Then a dog attacked and savaged a small child. She died of her injuries in hospital. I was held partially responsible."

"What?!" I cried. "What happened?"

"It turned out that the owner had been starving and beating the dog. An unlicensed Rottweiler incidentally. Then it escaped out into the street one day, and the child just happened to be the first thing it ran into."

"But surely the fellow who owned the dog was to blame in that case?" G. asked. "It makes no sense to blame you if he wasn't even following your advice."

"Well so I thought, but a copy of my book was found in his house, and certain of the papers fixed on that. The public lost all faith in my dog-training courses and I was forced to file for bankruptcy."

"I'm sorry to hear that," I said, putting a hand on her shoulder. "We can see the level it has brought you to."

"Oh no! I rebuilt myself as a business consultant."

G. clapped a hand to his head. "Of course! The Watkins System! I do remember! Very widely publicised as a fool-proof business plan for any size of enterprise!"

Miss Watkins smiled. "Ah, yes. That was our motto." Her face fell and she heaved a deep sigh.

G. didn't notice. "Drove half a dozen companies bankrupt as I recall. Horrible mess! The papers had a field d... Oh. I see."

Miss Watkins' shoulders slumped. "And not one of them followed my instructions, and I still got the blame."

The four of us stood in awkward silence. Monty didn't. He went and urinated rather noisily on a nearby hedge. I glared at him and thought of 50,000 volt shock collars.

"But!" she said, breaking the quiet, "I have a new plan! A new system to help people. And this time it will be so simple and straight forward, and so obviously sensible that people will have to follow it to the letter! You'll see, soon I'll be back on top again, and this time it will be to stay!"

And with this determined declaration, she squared her padded shoulders and marched onwards without so much as a wave or a backwards look.

We watched her until she disappeared out of sight. Then, sighing and shaking our heads at the follies of the world, we continued on our way.

The rest of the day passed without incident, if you exclude B. almost tripping over Monty, and as a result giving him a hefty kick 'by accident, he was in front of my foot you see'. I saw it as a dose of divine justice and it was only by an effort of superhuman will that I kept a smug grin off my face. I noticed G. glancing at me to register my reaction, but I gave him a carefully mild look, and so it passed without too much recrimination. B. refused to apologise to the dog though, despite G.'s urgings.

Chapter 17

On the concept of the Trinity.

The day was beginning to wane, but we were very nearly at our destination. We had booked spots in a camp site not too far off and we pushed on through a little village as the sun began to sink below the horizon.

As we walked through, weary at the end of a day's slog, we passed a pub. Light shone from the windows, and music and laughter drifted out to us on the lonely pavement. I stared mournfully at that pub, which in that instant appeared to me to be the very pinnacle of attainable happiness. I so wanted to be in that pub with a pint of beer before me. I ached to go inside and drink in the camaraderie and ambience of that delightful little country pub, along with its cool, nut-brown ales and deep, dark porters.

However, despite the deep, wistful yearnings of my innermost soul, I took full control of my being, and forced myself onwards, one cold, lonely step at a time. Suddenly, behind me the door opened, and for a brief, wonderful moment, I thought that the barman had heard the call of my spirit, looked through the window, seen my wistful glance and come out to me, beer in hand. Sadly not.

It was instead an older gentleman, who despite the

comparatively early hour was quite clearly tighter than a ballet dancer's girdle. He saw me looking and waved cheerily.

"Y' a'right there?"

I waved back perhaps a little half-hearted.

"Lovely night ain't it?"

I paused. The fellow wished to chat, and since it was indeed a pleasant evening, I saw no reason to hurry. Besides, I thought, if I could make G. and B. stay in the vicinity a while longer, one of them might suggest that we nip in for a quick pint.

"Yes, gorgeous." It was too. There wasn't a cloud in the sky, and now that the sun had dipped beneath the silhouette horizon the first stars were coming out, and a cool breeze had picked up to stir the trees into whispered conversation. I glanced up at the stars and took a deep breath. G. and B. had now noticed that I had stopped and stood waiting for me.

The fellow followed my gaze upwards and nodded. "Very pretty. But there's scary stuff up there too y' know."

"Oh yes," I agreed, "black holes, supernovas, dark matter. Really puts one in one's place thinking about it all."

"Oh, all that too, but I meant the aliens."

I did not look down at him. I continued to stare up at the heavens, but I did heave a deep sigh. It seemed as though we were physically incapable of going anywhere and talking to anyone without them turning out to be a crank of the worst possible kind. Where on earth were all the sane, normal people?

"Go on," I said with another resigned sigh. "What aliens?"

"Alien, I should say. I only saw one."

"And what did this interstellar apparition look like? Standard grey skin, big eyes, short legs sort of a job I take it?"

"Nothing like. No, it was a sort of... blob... thing."

I finally condescended to look down at him. "A sort of blob thing? It had a flying saucer I suppose? Or did it fall out of the sky like a meteorite?"

"It had a space ship. Sort of saucery, yes. Then this door opened and the... thing came out. It was the weirdest job I've ever seen. The alien that is. He floated above the ground. Just a big blob of... stuff. Kind of like liquid. Or maybe light. It glowed anyhow."

"When did you see this creature?"

"Not six months ago. I was on me way home from the pub. It was about one in the morning, and I'd just been sick in the ditch."

I nodded. "I see."

The chap frowned. "Here though, I wasn't drunk! Not very drunk anyway. I mean, I could still see. And walk. Sort of. But still not that drunk!"

"Of course not. And this floating liquid-light-blob wanted to meet your leader perchance?"

"No! If yer going to make fun of me I won't tell yer."

"I am all ears my good fellow, as this intergalactic sightseer also was no doubt, if he wasn't all teeth and tentacles. Now what did this beastie say?"

"Hello."

I blinked. "Hello? What, just 'hello'? That's not very dramatic is it? If I were to open dialogue with a whole new species, I'd have chosen something of a little more moment."

"Yeah, but then he said hello again."

"Had you replied?"

"Well no. I was staring at a glowing blob-thing alien! I was a bit speechless!"

"Perhaps it thought that you hadn't heard."

"Yeah, but that time I answered. Only it said hello four more times."

"It said hello to you six times?"

"Yep. Then it asked how we all were."

"All of you? Who else was there?"

"No one, just me and the blob."

"How curious. Perhaps you were so drunk it was seeing several of you?"

"Nah. 'Cos then it said, 'Which of you is the leader here? I wish to speak to them'.

"So 'take me to your leader' then?"

"Uh, s'pose so then, yeah. Well I looked around, but there was just me, so I scratched my head. Then it said, 'You are travelling together? Why do you scratch at the round one, long one? Are you the leader perhaps?'"

"Hang on, it was talking to your arm?"

"That's what it sounded like. It makes sense I suppose. It was just a single round... um, blob. It looked at me, and thought that I was a group of creatures all travelling together."

"Well that makes sense," I said, nodding. "For a being with only one part, that didn't know about limbs, it would probably seem like each part of you was moving and acting independently of the others."

"Yeah, I figured that out eventually, I told it that I was just one thing."

"And how did it take that?"

"I think it got confused. It said, 'But each of you is doing something different. The long, flat-bottomed ones are carrying wide-one (bloody cheek!), and wide-one is carrying thin tentacle-head ones and round, hairy, holed one. You all seem to have different functions. How can you be one being?'

So I told him that he was just seeing different parts of me, each doing its own thing, but that actually they were all me, and it was just me as one creature doing my own thing."

"Which was being sick in a ditch."

"Um, yeah."

"So it understood about you and your limbs and vomitousness?"

"Dunno. It floated back into its saucery thing and flew off."

"Leaving you and your vomit?"

"Yeah. I threw up again after that, then I felt a bit better so I went home to have another drink."

"I see. A close encounter indeed. I shall keep a wary eye on the skies tonight then."

"You do that. Good night."

I bid him a good night and caught up with my friends.

"What was all that about?" G. asked as I approached.

"Nothing. Just a man telling me about his vomit, and the curious effect alcohol has on the imagination." I glanced up at the star-strewn darkness and thought I saw a speck of light moving across it. A shooting star no doubt. A shooting star that could suddenly stop and change direction.

I shivered. "Let's get to that campsite then shall we?" I suggested, and set off at a brisk pace.

Chapter 18

On an Interventionist God and the nature of miracles.

That night, we bedded down in our tents and made a reasonably pleasant night of it. The air was warm, the campsite was well-situated and the weather was dry. Even Monty seemed able to forego his usual devilments and diabolicalness and sat at G.'s feet for most of the evening. I kept a wary eye on the stars, but saw nothing untoward, if being able to see thousands of nuclear explosions, each one larger and older than the planet that you're currently standing on can be described as 'untoward'. At least, I could see nothing unusual.

We rose early the next morning to find that the sky had clouded over, and that the day was quite humid. We made a swift but passable breakfast and began the day's slog.

We were now drawing into close proximity with the target of our mighty quest, and I half-expected to glimpse the far-off tower of Canterbury Cathedral every time we rounded a corner. Alas, each time I was to be disappointed.

However, upon turning another corner of a pleasant but somewhat remote country back-road, we came across a car in a visible state of disrepair. A column of blue-grey smoke rose from the bonnet and the sound of hissing steam was clearly audible.

A man sat on the grass verge next to one of those collapsible yellow hazard triangle things that drivers are supposed to carry round with them. He heard us approaching, looked up and gave us a wry smile.

"Good morning."

"Good morning," we all replied cordially.

"Are you alright there?" I asked, nodding towards the smoking vehicle.

"Oh yes, I've phoned the AA. They should be here in an hour or so."

"Quite a wait," I replied sympathetically.

"I don't mind really. It's a pleasant enough day, and it's quite nice to just sit and do nothing for a while."

We all nodded, the three of us being accomplished idlers of long practice.

"In fact," said the unfortunate motorist, "it's given me time to think about things."

"Oh? Pondering the nature of the universe and whatnot?"

"Something like that. I was thinking about engines."

"Ah, well that's natural really," B. said, "what with yours blowing up and all."

"Well yes, but I was rather wondering what the various components of the engine felt about it all."

B. frowned at this. "What, the break down? I expect that they're rather cross about it. Probably rather upset that one of their own has bitten the bullet."

"That's what I thought, but not just the breakdown. I meant the very existence of the engine itself. 'Here we are,' they must be thinking, 'in our nice, ordered world, each doing our allotted job according to the rules and laws that our world is based on. Surely the world must have been made specifically for us, and we for our world. We don't know what the point of the world is,' they only being engine parts, and not aware of the world outside the bonnet, 'but surely there is a point.'"

"Ah," I said. "You're wading into deep waters there. My friends and I have paddled in that direction ourselves."

He merely nodded at this and continued in his unsolicited philosophical monologue.

"That there is a point is perfectly apparent to them, but what that point might be is so utterly beyond their ability to experience and consider that they almost might as well not consider it at all."

"But surely," G. interrupted, "in that case, they really are better off not giving it a second thought, and just getting on with their oily little existences."

"Possibly, except that they do know that there is something out there, because it has entered into their world in such a way as they were able to experience it."

G. paused. "You've lost me there. How do you mean?"

"I'm referring to the intrusion, or perhaps superimposition, of the invisible world onto the visible by way of miracles."

G. snorted. "Miracles!" he scoffed. "And pray tell what miracles occur in the world of Engine?"

"Well, not so long ago, one of the components in the engine stopped working. It clogged up and died. I am no engineer, but even I could see that it simply wanted cleaning out, so I pulled it out, cleaned it up and put it back in again. I tried the engine, and lo and behold, it started up as good as new."

"Very sensible," B. put in. "It's always best to have a go

yourself before sending it to a garage. A long time ago, I was going to send my car to a garage, but decided to give it a look myself, and it turned out that it was simply a rat that had blocked it all up. I yanked it out and fed it to G's last dog."

G. glared at him suspiciously. "How long ago?"

"Oh, a week or two before the old chap died I think. Why?"

G. said something under his breath that I did not quite catch. I didn't bother asking him to repeat it. There are some things that one simply does not wish to hear.

"But anyway," our new acquaintance continued, "to the denizens of the Engine World, that component had been brought back from the dead. An agency that they had no ability to experience or comprehend had reached into their world and acted upon it in a mysterious way."

"A sort of Lazarus carburettor you mean?" I asked.

"Yes, I suppose so."

"But why," G. asked, "must that be a miracle? If such a thing is possible, why doesn't that happen all the time? It seems to me that any world, including the Engine World, would be far more enjoyable for its inhabitants if everything was directly taken care of by the unseen driver."

"Ah, but it is in the nature of Engine World that as parts are used they become dirty, they wear down and eventually they break. It's true that if all I ever did was clean the various components of my engine, it would be much better for them, but if I did that I, and by extension they, wouldn't ever get anywhere at all. They would not be worth having, and since they exist solely to make my engine work in the way in which it was intended, they would have no reason to exist either."

We wished him luck, bid him a good day and headed on down the road, each of us pondering the conversation.

Chapter 19

Speculations on the Afterlife, and the nature of body and soul.

There was that scent of tin again, and I waited with some impatience to discover what the result of the painful process would be. I heard B. take a breath, and I pricked up my ears, ready to fly in with a clever answer or cutting put-down, whichever seemed easiest or most appropriate.

"I think," said he eventually, "that the soul must be very much like a peanut."

I accepted this silently, thought about it for a few seconds, and finally shook my head. "Sorry old thing, I'm not seeing it."

"Perhaps some people are allergic to them?" G. suggested.

I nodded. "Or you could mash them up and make a delicious sandwich filling?"

"Or perhaps they are better dry-roasted."

"No, no, no, that's not at all what I meant," B. snapped impatiently. "I meant that the soul is like the nut, and perhaps the body is rather like the shell."

"I'm still not quite following you, sorry."

"Well it's like this. It seems to me that the shell is actually not really required by the tree, or bush or whatever peanuts grow on. What the tree's after is the kernel. That's the good bit that is intended for greater and longer term things. Same with us. We don't want the shells. We're after the bit that can be roasted, or buttered or whatnot."

"But if the tree didn't need the shell, it wouldn't have evolved it. Nature abhors waste you know," G. said firmly. "If it wasn't absolutely required, peanuts would not need shelling, which would actually be dashed convenient now that I think about it."

"You are missing my point, and I think you're doing it deliberately," B. sniffed. "I shan't go on if you don't listen properly."

G. contrived to look contrite. "I am sorry, do go on."

"As I was saying, what is wanted is not the shell, but the nut. The kernel that is. As you say, it would seem very convenient not to have to bother with the shell, and go straight onto the tasty bit without the hard and awkward bit, but without the shell, the kernel simply couldn't develop. It would dry up, or else be eaten by something long before it reached its full potential."

This seemed to make sense to me. "You're saying that the hard and inconvenient bit is required in order to allow the thing inside, which is the thing we actually want, to grow and develop?"

"Yes, that's more-or-less it. And I might extend the analogy to say that the harder, stronger and more inconvenient the shell is to crack, the better the nut is inside, since it's had far more opportunity to develop. And the better it will taste when you finally get it out."

The three of us nodded at this little piece of unexpected sagacity.

"And do you know what else I think?" B. asked after a

while. We looked at him in polite expectation.

"I think that all that talk of nuts has made me hungry. Is there a pub nearby?"

Chapter 20

On denominations and the purpose of the Holy Spirit.

There was indeed a pub nearby, and soon the three of us were sitting in relaxed repose, sipping at our glasses of cool beer. B. had also bought a packet of peanuts, having given himself a vicious craving with his little mental exploration.

I held my beer up to the light, watching the tiny bubbles rise slowly to the surface through the translucent red-brown liquid. I glanced at my companions' drinks. B. had a light lager of foreign descent, which he was attacking with gusto, and a small moustache of froth. G. had a pint of stout which he was approaching more cautiously, but with no less enjoyment. I settled for a red-hued bitter, hoppy and fruitful and absolutely the thing I needed.

"I say, you chaps?" I said, after a moment's thought.

G. looked at me. "Yes?"

"Do you not think that the whole thing's a bit like beer?"

"Which whole thing?"

I waved my hand vaguely. "The whole... religion thing. The church thingy."

"You mean if you have too much at once you make yourself ill?"

"Or perhaps," B. said, "if you take it in too quickly it causes gas?"

"No, neither of those. I mean that there are lots of different kinds, and to an outsider they might look like they're completely different. But in reality, they're all basically beer aren't they?"

The other two nodded in cautious agreement.

"I mean, I personally can't stand lager, and I don't mind stout too much, but what I really like is a decent pint of bitter. G. loves his stouts and porters, but cannot abide lager, and B. can swill the stuff back like water, but anything dark makes him come over all seedy."

They nodded again, still reluctant to follow too closely in case I went off on a sudden tangent. They were like feral cats being tempted by a proffered bowl of cat-food, willing to take what was offered, but ready to bolt the second I made a funny move.

"And they all taste very different don't they?" I continued, determined to persevere. "Lager and bitter and pale ale and porter and stout all taste and look slightly different, although some are more similar than others. But ultimately, they're all of the same kind, and all achieve the same effect in the end."

"Refreshment in small quantities, and drunkenness when taken too far?" G. suggested.

"I suppose so, yes. I'm not sure how far down that route I want to go at the present, but yes, that's what I'm getting at."

"So which is which?" B. asked, scratching his head.

"I don't know. I suppose that maybe Catholicism is stout, all heavy and dark, but full of flavour and nutriment to those who like the taste, whereas the C of E is more like bitter, full of endless variations on a single close theme. Possibly the lagers are the charismatic, evangelical ones, full of bubbles and bounce, but lacking any real depth or flavour."

"Well that works very nicely then," B. said firmly. "I can't stand stout, and Catholicism is certainly not for me."

"Oh? How come?"

"I have a bad history with Catholicism. I got taken along as a boy, and one week I was asked to help with some of the prayers. Only, at the time we were doing Robert Burns in school, and I was rather nervous and got the Hail Mary mixed up with Ode to a Haggis. They didn't want me back after that."

G. frowned bemusedly at him. B. shrugged. "Well you know, they start the same way. So I ended up saying 'Hail Mary, full of grace, Great chieftain o'the pudden race.' And by then it was too late and I had to keep running with it. As I say, I wasn't allowed back after that. They thought I'd done it on purpose."

"Yes, well, my point really was that when it comes to beer there's a great deal of snobbery and repugnance from all sides about the varieties that they dislike, but we forget all too often that we are all bound together in the great brotherhood of beer-drinkers and that we all share a common cause and a common goal. It's something to bear in mind before we sneer at girly lager drinkers or bearded and bellied real-ale types. In the end, we're all just here for the beer."

At this point, a fellow came in and headed over to the bar to order a drink. As he got to the bar, some electronic device or other went off in his pocket, beeping and buzzing away. It gave him quite a start, and he fumbled around trying to fish it out. Eventually he found it and silenced its racket. He looked at the screen and nodded. He turned and glanced around the otherwise empty pub until his eyes alighted on us.

"Can I offer any of you gentlemen a drink?"

We glanced at each other, sorely tempted, but we still had our own to finish, and the day was wearing on.

"No, but thank you very much for the offer."

He seemed relieved, and ordered his own drink before coming to sit on the table next to ours. He took a deep swig of his drink when suddenly his pocket beeped very loudly, making him jump. He started coughing and spluttering on his beer and had to wait for the fit to stop before he could turn off the little gadget.

He looked at the screen and nodded with a sigh.

"Um, did any of you chaps drop a tenner outside? I found it on the floor."

We checked wallets and pockets and came to the conclusion that the money did not in fact belong to any of us, and we told him so. He nodded, got up and went to the bar, where he deposited it in a charity box by the till. He came and sat back down and went back to his drink.

After about a minute of silence, which the three of us spent glancing at each other with no small amount of bemusement, we all jumped as the thing started its dreadful noise again. The fellow struggled with his pocket, dragged it out and turned it off. He checked the screen again, and nodded once more.

He got up, came over to our table and sat down. He smiled at us.

"So, have you gentlemen come far?"

"Oh, well, you know. Not very far really," I replied. "You?"

"I live quite close by. Just down the road."

"Ah, I see."

He eyed our rucksacks and tents. "You're camping I see."

"Um, yes. Yes, we're on a hike."

"Oh yes. Anywhere nice?"

"Canterbury."

"Oh right? Nice place, especially this time of year." He paused, and we sat in silence for a few seconds. "Nice weather we're having at the moment..." he began valiantly, but even this brave sally seemed rather forced.

An awkward silence ensued, which G. broke suddenly by asking, "What on earth is that thing that keeps going off in your pocket? Smartphone of some sort is it?"

He took it out and put it on the table. "What, this? No, it's something I've invented. Very clever thing really."

We nodded and looked at him expectantly.

"It senses what's going on around me and lets me know what I should be doing. It tells me what's right and how I should act."

"You mean that little box is telling you what to do?" G. said, sounding quite affronted. "You're allowing some mindless little electronic machine to order you around?"

"Well not exactly..."

"I think it's horrific! The idea that you would sublimate your natural free will to some inhuman and unhuman *thing* is abhorrent in the extreme. It makes you less than a man, nothing more than a highly developed automaton. Worse you allow it to take away from you the decision as to what is and is not morally right!"

"Ah, no, I think I've explained myself badly," the man said. "It doesn't tell me what is and isn't good, nor am I forced in any way to do as it suggests. It serves to remind me that there is always a more perfect way. Having being reminded, I can then decide for myself whether or not I am going to follow that more perfect way, and since I am trying my utmost to be a good person, I have almost always followed its advice. It does not command, it inspires. Whether or not I follow that inspiration is entirely up to me."

We left the pub in a thoughtful mood.

"One thing about that chap," B. said as we left.

"What's that?" I asked.

"His box didn't help his grammar. 'More perfect'?' Very poor. Very poor indeed."

Chapter 21

The foolishness of blaming God for failing to answer prayers.

That night, we camped again, pitching our tents in a small field just off the road. We dined on tinned articles of uncertain provenance, and lay for a while staring at the awesome and majestic spread of stars, stretching across the heavens above us. We said little that evening, and at some unmarked but mutually agreeable juncture, we took ourselves to our sleeping bags.

I lay there silently as I slowly warmed up, and gradually began to drift off. I drifted, nine tenths asleep, thinking over the various encounters that the three of us had had over the last few days, and pondering their significance. I wondered if there were not perhaps lessons to be learnt concealed within them, and indeed in every event of every day, and as I thought, I suddenly felt my heart strangely warmed.

It was a tricky feeling to describe to be honest. It was a gentle but deep and comforting warmth that centred on my chest. I felt the stirrings of a soul-filling eternal peacefulness spreading through me. I breathed a deep sigh of contentment, my chest rising and falling.

The source of the warmth wuffled grumpily and turned

over.

"G.!" I yelled as a Monty-scented streak bolted out of my tent, "I swear that I will turn that dog into the world's ugliest doorstop if you don't keep it away from me, do you hear!?"

As I went to sleep, I determined to start setting bear traps outside my tent every evening, and hoped I would remember to buy some the next day.

∽

The next morning came around without any more canine-related incidents, but I gave Monty a very fierce glower when I saw him in the morning. He replied by winking at me and wagging his tail. The sheer bare-faced brass of the beast was nothing short of infuriating, and a boot was about to be hurled when G. emerged, tousled and dishevelled. In the interests of peace and friendly cooperation, I withheld the boot, and gave him another prize-winning glare.

Having breakfasted and packed up our camp, we headed onwards, the morning breeze still cold against our backs.

The morning was pressing on when we saw a figure approaching us along the road. I thought at first that he was quite a considerable way off, but to my confusion, as he approached he didn't seem to get much larger, and was suddenly right in front of us without having grown appreciably in size.

The three of us stared in astonishment at the small child who trudged purposefully along the road. He was, so far as I'm any judge of such things, about four or five years old, and stopped when he saw us, staring at us without fear or hesitation.

"Have you got any food?" He asked after a moment's

thought. "I'm hungry."

B. dug into his bag and pulled out half a packet of biscuits, which he handed over. The lad tucked in with a vengeance, and soon all that was left were a few crumbs and the empty packet, which he handed back.

"Um, where are your parents?" I asked him. "Are you lost?"

The boy shook his head. "At home," he answered simply. "And I'm not lost. I ran away."

We looked at each other. "That's very brave of you," G. said, "but not terribly clever. Who's going to feed you? You can't expect everyone you come across to give you biscuits."

The young fellow frowned at this and nodded. "They can give me other things then. Don't always want biscuits."

"But what if you don't find anyone to give you anything? What will you do then?"

The boy shrugged. "Don't care. I don't need food."

"I'm afraid you do young lad. I'd turn around straight away and go back to your parents if I were you."

"No! I'm not going back to them!"

The three of us glanced at each other again. "Well why on earth not?" I asked.

"They hate me!"

"They hate you? Are you sure? Parents tend to love their children by and large."

"No! They hate me, so I ran away."

"But what makes you think that they hate you?"

"We were in a shop, and I saw a toy I wanted, and they wouldn't buy it! I *said* please!"

"Perhaps they couldn't afford it?"

"But I said please! And I was good. I was good all day, and I said please lots of times and they still didn't buy it.

They hate me, so I ran away."

"Now look here my lad, if I were you I would head home straight away. It seems to me that your parents love you very much."

"Then why didn't they buy me the toy?"

"Because sometimes what you want isn't always what you need. Your parents are much wiser than you child, and know that sometimes it is better for you not to have something. It might seem to you to be something that you very much need, but they see through and passed such shallow needs to the true things."

"But I said please. And I would have said thank you. I would have said it very nicely."

"I have no doubt of that whatsoever, but it isn't your parents' business to earn your gratitude. It's their business to fit you up for life. It isn't always possible or beneficial for you to get what you want all the time, even if it seems a perfectly reasonable or necessary thing that you're asking for."

"That's not fair though!"

"Fair? I don't really know about fair. What is and isn't fair isn't always the same as what is and isn't right, or good for you. I know it seems hard lad, but what your parents are doing, they are doing out of love for you, and out of a desire to see you become better than you are, perhaps even a hope that you will become as good as you were always meant to be. And I'm afraid that accepting these lessons is part of that, even if you don't understand them at the time."

The little boy thought about this for a while. "So you think I should go home?"

The three of us all nodded. "That would be a very good idea, "B. said solemnly.

Suddenly, a car appeared round a corner up ahead and rushed towards us. It stopped with a squeal of brakes, and a young couple spilled out of it. The woman grabbed up the boy and enveloped him in a suffocating hug.

The man ran round the front of the car and hugged them both. From inside the crush came the muffled voice of the child.

"Mummy, I want to go home now. I don't mind about the toy anymore."

Without words, but giving us an exceptionally eloquent look of gratitude, the parents ushered their boy into the car, and drove off into the distance.

We stood and watched it until it disappeared back round the corner.

"I think," G. said, "that if we do nothing else today, it will still have been a good day's work."

B. and I nodded, and after a few more minutes, we set off once more.

Chapter 22

On the nature of evil.

The rest of the day passed without any other incident, and we made excellent progress. However, as the day progressed heavy clouds billowed in from somewhere or other, and a light drizzle began to fall.

It continued for most of the afternoon, and stopped as night came on. Indeed, as it began to grow dark, the clouds disappeared completely, leaving the star-strewn sky arcing above us. Even though it was the height of summer, the night was growing frightfully cold, or at least it felt so to our softened, city-dwelling skins. Now, I am no meteorologist, but it was once explained to me that clouds are very much like a good thick duvet when it comes to keeping the planet warm, and that cloudless nights tend to be much the coldest.

The person who had explained it thus was bang on the money in this case, and as the sun went down, so did the temperature. Alas there were no handily nearby pubs or B&Bs, and besides our funds were beginning to run a little low. Too much time spent in pubs and not enough time spent walking and getting in some really good pilgrimming if you ask me.

As it was, we located a convenient field and put up our

tents, our trousers soon soaked through from the soggy ground. The evening only grew colder, B. and I set to building a fire while G. located the matches and fire-lighters.

B. and I soon had a nice little pile of dryish wood and grass built up, and we looked to G. expectantly. He had the box of fire-lighters out, and was rummaging around in his rucksack for the matches. Minutes passed; we continued to look and he continued to rummage, starting to swear under his breath.

"Not to rush you or anything old thing," I said eventually, "but it really is getting quite nippy. Don't you go believing all those things they say about global warming and greenhouse gases."

"Yes, yes, hang on. They're here somewhere. I'm sure of it."

We waited. He rummaged. We waited a little longer. It may have been summertime, but it was still deuced chilly, and I began to shiver. B. is gifted with rather more insulation than myself and didn't seem to mind so much, but I am built for hotter climes. 'Gracile' is what I am; evolved and adapted for the fast chase across the sun-soaked plains of a more southerly continent, built on the lean economy of the wolf. B. was more of a seals and huskies, igloo-building type, built on the lean economy of the walrus. Favourable volume to surface area ratio and whatnot. Small ears. 'Robust', the polite word is. G. falls somewhere in between, suited for the temperate climate between pole and tropic, and seemed as little troubled by the temperature as B.

"Blast and confound it!" G. snarled eventually. He turned to us. "I can't find them."

"Not at all?"

"Not even one lone, solitary match. We must have left

them at the last campsite."

"Don't you 'we' us! You were in charge of the matches, and if you forgot them then it is your fault! Don't go trying to spread the blame now! If I die of pneumonia I'll come and haunt you forever!"

"At least we still have the fire-lighters..."

I glanced hopefully at them. "I don't suppose they'll do the job by themselves?"

He shook his head. "If we have matches, they'll burn like hellfire. If not, they're singularly unlikely to burst into flame."

I sniffed. "Disgraceful! That's what it is! They shouldn't be allowed to go round calling them 'fire-lighters' when they do nothing of the sort! They should call them 'fire-improvers', or 'fire-expediters' or something. But when they do not light fires, they should not be allowed to claim that they do. There are laws against that sort of thing!"

G. nodded glumly and sat down next to me. The wind started to pick up a little, as though aware of our difficulty and determined to kick us while we were down. I shivered and pulled my jacket closer around myself. I wondered if G. would let me tape Monty's mouth shut, and affix his legs to his sides and use him as a (admittedly rather smelly) hot-water bottle. I decided that he would not.

G. started to shiver a little as well, and even B. zipped up his coat and hugged himself. Monty snuggled up closer to G. and the four of us sat there in silent misery for some time as it grew darker. B. got up and fetched some more sticks from the hedge, which he started rubbing together.

G. and I watched the sticks closely, ready for them to burst into flame. After a bit of rubbing, some of the bark fell off them. Then one of them broke suddenly and B. ended up stabbing himself in the hand. He gave a yelp and dropped both sticks. He grabbed them with a curse and hurled them away. Monty looked after them as though considering fetching them back out of sheer spite, but obviously decided that it was too cold even for that.

Then B. glanced out into the gathering night and paused. He squinted hard. "I say you fellows. Isn't that a fire?"

We followed his gaze and saw, across the field, a tiny, flickering spark. We stared and it seemed to grow a little brighter.

"I do believe you're right there, B. old chap. That does indeed seem to be a fire." I said.

"Do you suppose that they'd let us borrow some of it?"

G. scratched his head. "Possibly. We could ask for a branch to bring back here to light our lot with. It'd get the fire-lighters..."

"Fire-improvers," I interrupted firmly.

"Yes, fire-improvers then. It'd get them going, and then we'd be well away."

"Right then," I said, jumping up, "let's go over to the neighbours and ask to borrow a cup of fire."

We crossed the field, and a most nasty, squelchy and murky job it was too. We just kept our eyes fixed on that little flame and ploughed ahead. We soon came to the far side of the field, and could make out another tent in the darkness, with a little fire blazing away quite happily in front of it.

A chap sat by the flames with a toasting fork in one hand, and the scent of cooking sausages came to us quite clearly through the night. My stomach reacted with a loud gurgle.

"Um, excuse me?" I called.

The fellow jumped a mile and stood up, looking in our direction. We advanced forwards into the firelight and I smiled at him.

"Hello there, we're camping on the other side of the field, and I'm afraid we…" I glared at G. at this point, "…have rather lost our matches. We couldn't borrow a bit of your fire to take back to light ours with could we?"

"Nasty night for camping isn't it?" he replied. "Why don't you just come and sit here with me for now? This fire's plenty big enough to warm up four of us, and I'm sure I'd be glad of the company."

We accepted this gracious offer, and sat down in a circle around the flame. The chap tossed on some more branches and the fire soon grew up to a very decent size, throwing out a good amount of heat. I could feel the warmth working its way through me, dispelling the cold that had crept into my bones.

We sat in appreciative silence for a while, staring into the flames. The fellow finished cooking his sausage and offered it to G., who accepted enthusiastically. The chap then put another three sausages onto the fork and began cooking them all at once. My mouth began to water heavily.

As the sausages began to bubble and hiss, the chap sighed and stared out into the deep darkness.

"I have always thought," he began, "that this is very much what the world is like."

"How do you mean?" I asked. "You mean mostly darkness? A tiny speck of light in a cold and uncaring void?"

"Yes, in a manner of speaking."

"You are, I take it, a pessimist then?" G. enquired.

"Oh, not at all! You misunderstand me. It's my opinion, although I can't claim any credit for the theory, since it's not a new one, that goodness is very much like light, or heat."

I frowned, vague recollections of blood-stained physics papers wavering in my mind. "It travels in waves?"

"No, no. Nothing like that!"

"In beams perhaps? I really didn't do too well with the electromagwotsit thingies."

"No! I meant that we define it by contrasting it with its absence."

There was silence as we chewed this one over, except for Monty, who made the most horrible guzzling noises as he savaged half of G.'s sausage. Not a great contemplator is old Monty. Not when there's sausage (or shins, sheep, sheets or shoes) to be mauled!

"It's like this," the chap tried again. "We tend to think of heat and cold as being opposites."

We nodded.

"But in actual fact, cold is not the opposite of heat. It is merely its absence. In terms of scientific fact, there is no such thing as cold. Merely the greater or lesser presence of heat."

"I'm afraid that I cannot agree with you there," B. said firmly. "I have been cold. I have experienced cold in a very real and positive fashion. I can tell you quite objectively that cold does indeed exist, and if you think it doesn't, just go and ask Captain Scott!"

The chap nodded patiently. "You're quite right that we are familiar with a sensation that our brains receive from our nerve endings and interpret as cold. However, our nerves are simply informing the brain that there is less heat in the air, less than the brain considers is good for the body, and therefore it interprets it as the unpleasant sensation of cold, for good, solid evolutionary reasons."

"And you," G. asked, "consider good to be very much of that nature?"

The man nodded.

"So you would say that there is no such thing as evil,

merely a greater or lesser presence of good?"

He nodded again. "That is correct."

"You wouldn't, for example, say that genocide or rape were acts of evil?"

"Of course I would."

"But I thought that evil didn't exist."

"It doesn't. You can freeze to death, and it causes the most agonising pain as it happens, or else the body goes completely numb and is unable to recognise either heat or its lack anymore. There is a cold so absolute that matter virtually ceases to exist at it. There are places and times where the near-total lack of good has numbed people. Entire nations. If there is a recognisable sensation that we call cold, then there is certainly a recognisable sensation that we can call evil."

"I see."

"Our nerves and our brains tell us that there is a thing called cold. Our knowledge tells us that there is not, simply that some things are less hot than others."

"That," G. said firmly, "sounds rather wishy-washy to me. Denying the presence of evil is simply to abdicate responsibility for dealing with it."

Our generous host shook his head emphatically. "I can see very well why you would say that but you're really quite wrong. Just because I know that cold does not exist in and of itself does not mean that I cannot freeze to death, and just because I know that darkness is merely the absence of light does not mean that I can't fall down a darkened staircase. I know that cold and darkness do not exist as entities, but that does not stop me from being able to warm myself and light my surroundings, and it certainly does not stop me from wishing to."

"Then despite what you say," I put in, "you really are a

pessimist if you think that people can achieve something close to the absolute zero of goodness."

"But I don't believe that at all! A human being can only exist within a tiny section of the heat spectrum. Exposed for any length of time to anything very much below zero, a man will soon die. Exposure to anything very much above say sixty degrees would achieve very much the same result. Absolute zero is -275 degrees. Imagine the depths of evil that would destroy a man instantly if he were exposed to them, sucking the very life from his body! Imagine the burning, all-consuming fires of good that would reduce him to ashes in a microsecond. No, I do not believe that humans have it in their power to be very evil, or even very good, but I do believe that we can still burn brightly for all that. The universe is a very cold and very dark place, and in the deepest darkness, even a very small light will be seen for a great distance all around."

Chapter 23

On blaming God for the existence of suffering.

The next morning, we rose bright and early, but discovered that the camper had already risen, struck camp and headed off. The field was no less squidgy than it had been the previous night, but thanks to the rapidly rising sun it was already a little warmer. We breakfasted (cold of course), struck our tents and continued on our pilgrimage.

We hadn't been going for very long at all when we found ourselves coming through yet another little village. We passed a small supermarket, complete with a car park. Only three or four cars currently rested here, but as I glanced at them, there was a sudden hiss and one of the cars shuddered and tilted very slightly.

The three of us paused and stared at the vehicle, and as we watched there was another hiss and the car most definitely listed to one side. As we looked, a man appeared and moved round to the front tyre of the side nearest us. He raised something in his hand, and I realised that it was a knife. With a vicious motion, he slashed the tyre, releasing the air within in a sudden hissing burst.

"I say!" I cried. "What the devil do you think you're

doing?"

The fellow jumped a mile, spinning round to look at us and trying somewhat ineffectually to hide the blade behind his back.

"Wh...what? What do you want?"

The three of us marched up to him. Now I'm not normally the sort to advance on a fellow armed with a knife, but there's safety in numbers and having a couple of stout fellows at your back (or if they're not available, G. and B.) gives one a most marvellous courage that would be absent if you didn't have your reputation to think of. Pride, although a sin most foul, does at least have the benefit of occasionally forcing one to be good, even when one's own inclinations are quite against it. I would say that having a dog along helped as well, but to be honest I doubt Monty would really have been much use in a stand-up brawl. All bark and no bite that one.

"What are you doing to that car, sir?" I demanded.

"What, this car?"

"That car there, sir. The one whose tyres you have just slashed."

"Oh no, no I didn't."

"Oh yes you did!" B. cried. "We saw you, you young rapscallion."

"Oh, um, yes but it's my car."

"Your car? Then why are you slashing its tyres?"

He drew himself up and raised his chin loftily. "I can do what the hell I like with my own property."

"But why do it in a car park and not at home, and why try to hide while you were doing it?" G. enquired mildly.

"Um... to... to avoid exactly this sort of embarrassing confrontation!"

"You have the papers for this car have you then?" I asked.

The chap opened and closed his mouth several times. "Fine!" he shouted. "Fine, I admit it! It's not my car! Happy? You have merely witnessed the first blow struck in my glorious crusade, my epic battle against the forces of evil!"

We were starting to get used to this sort of thing by now, so we simply waited politely for him to get on with it. This seemed to rather throw him off his stride and he waited for several seconds for a question that did not come.

"Uh, yes! My crusade against the murderous engine of destruction that is the automotive vehicle!" He paused and looked at us expectantly. I smiled encouragingly and gestured for him to continue. "Right, yes. Well then. So that's why I've slashed the tyres of this car. Which isn't actually mine. That was a lie. Sorry. But I've done it to save lives!" he added, trying to rally himself.

"How will that save lives then?" G. asked, obviously willing to help the chap along.

"Do you know how many people are killed on our nation's roads every year by cars and lorries and motorcycles? The dozens of loves snatched away in their primes? The children left orphaned? The grey-haired old ladies who wait with patient serenity for sons and daughters and grandchildren who are never again to brighten their lonely old age?"

I frowned, puzzled. "Well yes, but almost all of those are accidental. I'm not trying to detract from the individual tragedy of each case, but surely you can hardly blame the cars for them?"

"I don't! Not at all. To blame these inanimate objects would be the height of insanity. No, I blame the inventor of the car. The man who first put an engine on a road-going vehicle. Surely that man was either evil or insane to produce such a device. What monster, what tyrannical mass-murdering genocidal fiend must that man have been?"

"But look here! That's not the purpose of the car at all. Mr Mercedes-Benz or Ford or whoever it was back in the day didn't think 'Today, I shall build a machine for running over little old ladies'. He thought, 'Today, I shall build a machine for rapidly transporting someone from point A to point B without having to bother with the railways'."

G. nodded vigorously. "Here, here! I agree that all the deaths and injuries are very bad, but they are merely unfortunate side-effects that result in the abuse of the car, not events naturally resulting from its correct use."

"Yes," I said, leaping back into the fray, "the car was invented with a single purely benevolent purpose in mind. However, for it to be able to fulfil its purpose, it must work in such a way as to allow it to harm those that it is meant to help. If a car is built in such a way as to allow it to carry a person sixty miles in an hour, it must also be built in such a way as to crash a fellow into a brick wall at sixty miles an hour as well."

"Yeah, but that's wrong!" he retorted. "It would be better for everyone if there wasn't a car at all."

"And everyone used the trains? You don't work for the railways do you?"

"They're next! Once I have driven the car from the road, no pun intended, I shall start on the train, slayer of innocents and butcher of humanity."

"So ultimately, you think that if travelling means the possibility, however slight, of injury or death, then you would rather not travel at all?"

He nodded. "That's right!"

My companions and I looked at each other. I looked back at the knife-wielding fanatic. "Well I simply cannot agree with you. It's true that the journey holds many risks, not least the risk of never getting to where you think you're going, but I would rather take those risks, and bear up under the slings and arrows of outrageous fortune, than never have begun the journey at all. Speaking of which, my friends and I have to get going. Good day."

With that we turned and left, heading into the little supermarket, where we informed the lad at the main counter what was happening, and advised him to phone the police.

Chapter 24

On doing as we would be done by.

Having alerted the young chap behind the customer service desk to the tyre-slashing madman outside, we decided that since we were in here, we might as well pick up some supplies for the road. Monty had managed to consume a large proportion of our sausage supplies, besides which bread and other victuals for the road were required.

We wandered the shop collecting such things, along with lots of others that we'd had absolutely no idea we desperately needed until we saw them on the shelves. I commented on this sudden and inexplicable urge.

"Mind control." B. said solemnly. G. and I looked at him sceptically. "No, really!" he insisted. "You know how the lights in these places aren't actually on all the time? They flicker very, very fast. That's why some people start to feel sick if they spend too long in supermarkets. Even though the eye can't detect the flickering, the brain does and starts to feel motion sick. Or something like that." He paused, struggling to remember his point. "Ah, yes! Anyway, the lights flicker in Morse code, and urge you to buy all sorts of things that you don't really want."

I pondered this for a second. "But I don't know Morse

code," I pointed out. "So how come my brain's understanding these subliminal light messages?"

"It's because," G. butted in before B. could answer, "his theory is complete and utter hokum. The real reason is those hot air thingies they have over the doors. As you step in, you get a blast of hot air to the top of your head. This overheats the brain and causes it to work less efficiently for a while. Now, in most cases, if your brain is reduced in efficiency by, say, twenty percent, this simply results in you buying an extra packet of biscuits, or suddenly deciding that you badly need a pork pie. In those of a more modest mental persuasion," and I swear he shot a glance at me as he said this, "it results in a severe loss of faculties. That's why otherwise perfectly rational, reasonable people turn into rude, easily confused simpletons, unable to read even the most simple labels or tickets. It's why I always wear a hat while entering a supermarket, to protect my thinking apparatus."

We had been wandering about the shop as he talked thus, and we turned into the next aisle to see a most extraordinary sight. One that I have, I should add, seen several times since.

A young chap in the livery of the shop was standing next to a metal trolley on which sat a strange device, something like an obese calculator. Next to it sat a little rectangular gadget, which as I watched spewed out a long row of stickers that the chap then applied to the items on the trolley. He would pick up the calculator thing and scan the barcode of an object with some sort of laser-wotsit at one end, tap in something on the buttons, and the little printer would spit out another sticker.

A small crowd of people, mostly elderly, were bunched round him, and as he stuck a sticker onto an object, one or more of them would snatch at it and thrust it into their basket.

Some were reaching for them even before the stickers were on. One old man seemed especially eager, keeping up a volley of chatter at the lad, smiling and nodding and thanking him in the most effusive terms whenever the fellow handed him a be-stickered item.

Getting closer, I could see that these stickers carried much-reduced prices, and the gaggle of people were snatching up these reduced items, whether out of poverty or simple bargain-hunting I couldn't say. Certainly some of them seemed to be getting rather greedy, their baskets over-flowing with objects as they grabbed for more.

The old man kept up his chatter to the rather harassed-looking assistant. "Ah, you're very good to me you know. You're a good friend. I shall tell your boss. I shall tell him what a good boy you are. You should get a promotion you know. Be boss of this place. Could you put that one down a bit more do you think? Much obliged, much obliged. Is that as cheap as it's going? No more? Just for me? No? Well I don't know! But you're good to me. That's all I think. Thank you Colin, thank you so much. You're a good friend to me. I shall see you tomorrow eh? Yes, see you tomorrow."

It seemed like the flow of cheapened items had ceased, and the group abruptly left, heading for the tills. The fellow heaved a deep sigh of relief, shaking his head. He turned and began to push his trolley back towards the back of the shop.

"I say," I said intercepting him, "that looked deuced wearing."

He gave a weary smile. "Oh, yes."

"And it happens every single day?"

"Like clockwork. Those are the things going out of date today. We knock them down in price to get rid of them."

"And don't you just!"

He shrugged. "As long as someone buys them, I suppose."

"And that old fellow comes in every day as well?"

The lad heaved a deep sigh and nodded.

"I'd have punched him the nose by now! You have the patience of a saint, old chap!"

He shrugged again. "I try to be patient with them. I'm not going to pretend that it's easy, but I've found ways of thinking about it that make it better."

"Oh? Zen breathing techniques? Catechisms against irritation, that sort of thing?"

"Not exactly. What I used to do was try and remember that there's always a chance that that old man is God in disguise. Coming here every day, doing the annoying little old man thing. It's not his fault he's the way he is, and he deserves to be treated with as much courtesy and respect as anyone else, and it's up to me to rise above myself and give him that. Even when it's very, *very* hard."

I nodded thoughtfully. "That's a very mature attitude you have there. Very moral. Very good."

He shook his head. "No, it isn't. I realised that I was completely wrong. I realised that trying to treat people as though they might be God in disguise is all very well, but it assumes rather a lot. It's basically a bit arrogant."

"Oh? So what do you do now?"

"That old man only talks to me when he wants something. He only goes on at me about how good I am and what a good friend I am and all that to try and persuade me to make things a little bit cheaper for him. He never talks to me for any other reason. Even when he's thanking me and saying nice things, it's in the hope that I'll treat him preferentially later. When I thought about it like that, I had a realisation that makes me try and treat him even better than ever."

"Oh? I'd have thought you'd treat him with contempt!"

"I certainly hope not. If I do then it leaves things looking very bleak for me."

"Why so?"

"Because I realised that that little old man isn't like God, talking to me. He's like me, talking to God."

క్ర

As we left, newly-laden with our groceries, I turned to the other two.

"You know, it's amazing where you find people who think about these things."

G. nodded. "They get everywhere. Like cockroaches in that respect. Widely spread and impossible to completely stamp out, no matter how hard they try."

I thought about that for a moment. "Good."

Chapter 25

***Of our inability to save ourselves, but the
ability to accept or deny salvation, and do
so more than once.***

We'd pushed on and left the village of the bizarre anti-car
chap and the unexpectedly theological shop-worker far
behind us. The day, which up till now had been so warm and
sunny, had slowly become more overcast and we soon began
to think of lunch. We had the food we bought from the
supermarket, and now all we wanted was some quiet, pleasant
place to sit down and enjoy it.

After another half an hour or so of walking, the hedge that
bordered the road to our left opened up and revealed a large,
placid pond, equipped with a couple of benches. On the far
side was a hut or shed of some sort, and next to it, at the
water's side were moored a number of small rowing boats,
presumably for hire. As we watched, one of these boats
drifted out with a man working awkwardly and most
inefficiently at the oars. A few ducks and a pair of swans sat
on the edge, and all looked at us as we appeared.

Monty saw them, and with an eager little bark scampered
towards them. One of the swans regarded him with
malevolent eyes as he gamely rushed towards them, yapping.

The ducks scattered, quacking fearfully, but as the little hound came up to it, the swan reared up, spreading its wings wide and giving a most ferocious hiss.

Monty came to a skidding halt and stared up at the enormous bird for a couple of seconds, his mouth open. Then he started yapping again, jumping up and down on the spot.

"Look at him!" G. said, his eyes bright. "He's so courageous! Come back here Monty!" he called. "Stop bothering that swan." Monty ignored him and continued to yap.

"He isn't courageous at all," I said firmly. "He's a cretin. He's so thick he doesn't know that he ought to be scared. Those things can break a man's arm. It could snap Monty in half without breaking a sweat." I paused and thought about this for a second. "Get him Monty!" I called to him. "Go on! Go for the throat!"

Monty continued his noisy but somewhat ineffective assault. The swan lowered its head and glowered at him, obviously bewildered by the lack of arms to break. Before it could come to a decision, G. stepped smartly forwards and scooped the diminutive mongrel up. Apparently the thought of seeing him broken in half had proved too much. As he was carried off, Monty stared wistfully at the swan. I had no doubt that upon returning to his regular haunts, his doggy friends would hear all about 'the one that got away'.

"Just as well Monty," B. said consolingly. "Those things belong to the Queen. You'd have been executed for treason or something."

I rubbed my chin and wondered if I could somehow arrange for Monty to be found over the corpse of a slain swan but before I could formulate any workable plan, my train of thought was interrupted by a yell and a splash.

I looked up to see that the fellow we'd seen in the rowing boat had somehow contrived to go overboard, and now he was thrashing around in the water in a blind panic. It was quite obvious that the chap could swim like a bowling ball.

I was just about to cast off my pack and coat and leap to the rescue, honest, when an old man appeared from inside the hut with a rubber life-ring in his hands, attached to a length of rope. He hurled it to the drowning man, who clutched at it for dear life. With strong heaves, the old chap brought the fellow to the edge of the pond and hauled him onto dry land.

Swans, treason and dead Montys all forgotten, we rushed over to see if we could help in any way. By the time we arrived, the unfortunate man was sitting up, spluttering a bit and trying to ring the pond-water out of his suit jacket.

"I say, are you alright?" I asked as we ran up.

He looked almost surprised. "Me? Oh yes, of course. No, don't you worry. Once I'd extricated myself from that little difficulty, I was quite alright."

"Extricated yourself? What about this heroic fellow here?" I asked, gesturing to the old man. "If it weren't for him, you be sleeping with the pond-snails!"

"What rot!" he snorted. "I saved myself. After all, it was me who hung onto the life-ring. I could have chosen not to you know!"

"But if this man hadn't thrown it to you, there'd have been nothing to hang on to!" I replied hotly, appalled by his ingratitude.

"There might be an argument there perhaps," he said lazily, "but I don't think it would hold water, no pun intended. Anyway, I think that's enough boating for today. Goodbye." With this, he picked himself up and sauntered off, leaving a trail of water behind him.

The three of us stared after him indignantly. "What a confounded idiot!" B. snarled. B. hates ingratitude as much as I do. Indeed, the effort to avoid its appearance may explain his generous proportions. When offered food, he hates to appear ungrateful.

The old man shrugged. "I get that sometimes," he said with a slight sigh. "It doesn't really matter. Just as long as I've got them out, that's the main thing really. And they always pay in advance."

"You mean to say that there's more like him?" G. asked, shocked.

"Oh yes. I've been here years and seen all sorts. If they go over the side, I can only throw 'em the ring. It's them that has to hold onto it. So some people are like that one, and think as they've saved 'emselves by holding onto it. Others don't see it at all and drown without ever knowing how close they were to living."

"How horrible!" I exclaimed. "How sad."

The old man nodded. "Oh yes. A great shame. There's some though who see the ring, and choose not to hold onto it. They'd rather try and learn to swim there and then and they all sink instead."

"How foolish!" G. murmured.

"Some of 'em realise what's happening before it's too late and grab the ring at the last possible moment, so I can pull 'em to shore, but lots drown instead. There are some indeed, who grab hold of the ring, but before they're halfway back to shore, they let go again and drown anyway."

"Utter folly!" B. said, aghast.

"Although even then there are some who realise how stupid they're being and grab it again in the nick of time. And then there are those who see it, know it for what it is and cling tightly to it all the way back to the shore. They're the ones who live. Most are grateful, and realise that although the choice to hold onto the ring or not was theirs, it was me who threw it, and me who hauls 'em in."

"You'd have thought," G. said with a frown, "that if you've been doing it so long, you'd be able to recognise which are the ones likely to let you save them and be grateful for it and which aren't, and then save yourself the bother of trying to save the ones who won't allow themselves to be saved."

The old man nodded and smiled. "Oh yes. I know all of the types. I've got so as I can recognise 'em on sight, I have. But it doesn't matter. I'll throw the ring out to all of 'em, good and bad alike. If they don't want to be rescued, well I won't make 'em hold the ring, but at the end of the day, they'll never be able to say that I wasn't ready to help if they'd wanted it. They'll never be able to say that the ring wasn't there to grab."

⌇

As we walked away from the pond, we heard a snuffling and growling from behind us. We turned to see Monty struggling to drag a dead duck along by its head. He saw us looking at him and stopped, staring up at us with his tail wagging.

"I don't suppose ducks are the property of the crown are they B.?"

"No, I don't think so."

"Hmph. Ah well, never..." Then a thought occurred to me. "I don't suppose she owns all the bras either?"

"All the bras? No, I think they're privately owned. Why?"

"Oh nothing. Shame though."

Chapter 26

On the diminishing need for God in a world of science.

We pushed on from the pond and its magnanimous owner, and had our lunch a little further along, next to a pleasant field of waving green grass. Having eaten, we set off once more.

We'd made an hour's good progress and were passing through another settlement when we heard a whirring noise behind us. We turned just in time to see one of those electric mobility scooter things bearing down towards us at a little under mach 1. The chap in the seat showed no signs of stopping, and we were obliged to make a leap out into the road as the contraption shot past.

Unfortunately, directly next to us was a deep puddle left from the recent showers and the three of us ended up splashing into it and soaking our boots. Monty, being a diminutive sort of hound almost disappeared before G. hauled him up by the lead and set him back up on the pavement. I immediately began to think more kindly of our near-destroyer. Then the water began to seep through my socks, and dissolved my benevolent thoughts.

We turned to glare at the fellow, who had slowed to a

mere walking speed in order to cross the road. He turned as he got onto the opposite pavement and then went back to warp-speed in a blur of geriatric mobility.

"Those things," G. proclaimed firmly, "are a public menace."

B. and I nodded. "I was hit by one of those in a shop a few months ago," I said ruefully. "Didn't half hurt my shin, I can tell you!"

"They should have to have a test before they're allowed out in one," B. said.

"Did you get a look at him?" I asked the others as we tried to shake the excess water off our boots.

"No. Why?"

"He didn't look all that old to me is all. He didn't look disabled either."

"It might have been something like severe arthritis," G. pointed out. "That wouldn't show from the outside."

"Huh. I reckon he was just lazy. Too lazy to get a bike out and do a bit of pedalling. And on the road!"

Still muttering about the stupidity and laziness of people in general, we pushed on, and presently came to a sort of cafe or tea-room where we decided to stop, take afternoon tea and give our feet a bit of a chance to dry out.

We went inside, ordered tea and scones, and sat down to our repast. Not five minutes had gone by when there was an electric whirr, and the red mobility scooter appeared and came to a sudden and screeching halt. The man riding it, whom, as I had observed, was only of middle-age, hopped off and came into the tea-room with no signs of concealed arthritis or another covert condition of any kind. I glanced at G. meaningfully, and he nodded, frowning.

"I bet," I said quietly, "that he sleeps with his feet by the headboard. I'm told that that's where the rot sets in."

The man obviously felt the force of our glowers on his back and turned to look at us. He took his cup of tea and walked over to us.

"I say, I passed you lot a few minutes ago didn't I?" He glanced at our rucksacks and (rather damp) walking boots. "Oh. You're walkers. How sad."

I sighed. Another one. "And what do you mean by that?"

"Oh, only that you're obsolete. Sorry, I know that sounds slightly offensive but it's true."

"Obsolete? It does indeed sound extremely offensive. I think you ought to explain yourself." I was starting to get quite cross. He had interrupted me in my tea-drinking, and G. and B. will both tell you that that is the swiftest way to tease my wrath.

"Look, back in the beginning, I'm sure that walking was all very well. It got you from A to B, eventually, and people didn't know any better. It was an age of innocence and ignorance."

"And what is so very wrong with that?" I demanded.

"Nothing really, not in itself," he said soothingly, "but there are better ways of doing things. I mean, it's acceptable for primitive peoples who don't know any better, and in the absence of anything else it certainly seems to make a sort of sense. Only then, mankind moved on. We domesticated the horse, and we found that by riding on that, we didn't have to walk as much."

"True, but most people couldn't afford horses, so walking was still what most people had to do." G. pointed out.

"Oh yes. The wealthy and educated could cast aside the primitive practice of pedestrian perambulation, but at some point, we invented the wheel, and created carts and carriages that could harness, quite literally in fact, the power of a single horse and allow it to transport several people at once, and often for only a very modest fee. And so it remained for a great many years. The rich had their steeds, and the merely well-off had their coaches and carriages, and the poor had their tired, thread-bare walking, already very much showing its age."

G. and I shared a glance. B. though, I noticed with some concern, was nodding quiet assent with this lunatic. The loony in question, however, was continuing so I had no chance to question my companion.

"Long centuries passed, and small improvements were made to the basic designs available. More comfortable saddles, carriages with suspension, but all still dependent on the motive power of the equine beast. Then, man invented the bicycle! No longer must the poor man choose between penury, and the humiliation of reverting to that wallow of primitive savagery that was walking. Men of science and technology had stepped in, if you will excuse the distasteful phrase, and heaved man up from the sinks of depravity. But this was not yet the greatest height to which our species was to aspire, oh not by a long shot. For then, the celestial, internal combustion engine was created. Only now did mankind become truly automotive, able to cast off forever the shackles on both body and mind that the execrable custom of walking imposed."

G. and I exchanged another very significant look. I drained my tea in a single gulp, and stuck what was left of my scone in my pocket for later. We were going to get up and leave, but B. was still sat there, a rapt expression on his face.

"So true..." he murmured.

"And now, at last..." our excitable new acquaintance

cried, getting really quite loud, "...we are freed from the necessity of walking even on the pavements and in the shops. Truly, are we at the zenith of our civilisation. We are in the Golden Age."

"B.," I asked, "are you actually agreeing with this frothing lunanaut?"

"But it's all so true!" B. cried. "And you!" he yelled, jumping to his feet. "You have dragged us out all this way, with your stupid spirituality and your... your *walking!*"

"Me? You can stop that again at once! I did not drag you out here, you agreed that it was a good idea."

"But that's before I knew how much walking it was going to involve," he wailed plaintively. "G. back me up on this one, there's a good fellow."

G. shook his head. "I can't honestly say that I'm entirely convinced by all this," he said, "but this chap here is clearly a pants-on-head rabid mentalite. You put all of this nonsense out of your head immediately and come with us."

"I most certainly shall not!" B. snapped, waving his finger in G.'s face. "I shall take myself, walking I must admit, to the nearest mobility shop, where I shall purchase one of these wonders of the modern world, and I shall never walk anywhere ever again, so long as I live!"

"Alleluia!" our crazy new acquaintance whooped. "Shout it from the rooftops brother!"

"B.!" I yelled, banging my hand down hard on the table. My portly companion started loudly and stared at me in astonishment. "Now listen here! This fellow is a nutter and an idiot, and I shall tell you why."

"Sounds sensible to me..." B. muttered sulkily.

"Nonsense! Now then, it's all very well to say that walking is an inefficient way of travelling. That may or may not be true, as it goes, I happen to think walking as humans do is a perfectly acceptable mode of transportation for everyday purposes." B. tried to interrupt me here but I would have none of it. I was immensely cross and the fact that my feet had not dried even slightly was having no calming effect on me whatsoever. "BUT," I continued loudly, "it's not for mere purposes of travel that we walk nowadays. It's true that we have more efficient, more 'scientific' ways of moving now, but there is an infinite amount more to life than the simple slog to and from work every day by the same route. A to B and B to A, day in and day out!

"Why, you ask, did I 'drag' you out on this expedition? We all agreed that it was a good idea, considering the state of ourselves, but you are of course correct. We could have driven. We could have taken the train. We did not. We chose to walk, and that is because it is good to walk, and good for us to walk. It is my firm belief that there is nothing more restorative to the human soul (besides tea of course) than walking alone through woods. You could cycle, you could even I daresay, use one of those electronic contraptions, but it would not be the same. You would move faster of course, but you would miss out on so much of what there is around you. Faster is not necessarily better, B. For as long as I live, I shall defy any man who tries to tell me that science has removed the need for me to wander through green glades, tarry by still pools, stride up steep hills with the wind in my hair and the bracken underfoot, stroll through sunny parks or amble down the quiet, hedgerow-lined lanes of England. I tell you this, those who think that they don't need such things, who think that they are obsolete and unnecessary, are something less than men, and their lives are something less than good. Just my opinion of course, but there you are."

I paused and lowered my head. "Come on then, G." I said quietly. "The fellow's made up his mind and it is not for us to stand in the way. Let's go and wear away some boot leather." G. nodded and we put our boots back on, B. watching us with a surly, sorrowful expression. We heaved our rucksacks onto our backs and left.

We had been walking for about two minutes when we heard footsteps behind us. "Wait up you fellows!" we heard B.'s voice cry. We turned and saw him hurrying after us as best he could, his boot-laces undone and his rucksack on one shoulder.

We waited for him to catch up. He stopped in front of us, puffing hard. He shrugged and smiled sadly. "I think you're right J.," he said. "I don't think one of those scooter things would suit me. It would rob me of my accustomed grace and poise as I saunter down the high street."

I smiled back at him. "My dear chap, your grace and poise were all I had in mind. Now let's hear no more of it."

As we walked away, I faintly heard a whirring noise which became suddenly high pitched and grating, followed by venomous but distant swearing. I couldn't suppress a slight smile and saw that G. was smirking too. It had been a sound almost exactly like that of a man trying to start a mobility scooter without realising that every single tyre is completely flat.

Chapter 27

On how science may not have removed the need for God, but may have removed the need for a Devil.

We tramped along in satisfied silence for a bit. The clouds were coming on again and, presently, it began to rain one of those warmish, gentle, sprinkling rains at which England is well-practised. The kind of rain that alights upon one's face with the gentleness of a feather, but which is capable of putting a chap from nought to soaked in about two minutes. The trickiest thing is that a fellow hardly notices that it's raining until he's sodden to the socks.

The three of us, however, were travellers and Englishmen of no mean experience, and we instantly recognised the first signs of a Stealth Soaker. Alas, there were no handy pubs to claim sanctuary in (for once!) so we had to settle for the green roof of a spreading oak that stood beside the road.

We had been standing there for only a very short time when we heard a grunt from the field behind us. Turning, we could see through a gate in the tall hedge, where we could make out a fellow heaving on something out of sight. A voice came from behind the hedge. "Pull!" The chap we could see dug his heels in and heaved with all his might.

The three of us looked at each other. "The local tug-o-war team practising perhaps?" I ventured.

"Come on! Pull!" the unseen speaker shouted again, and the chap redoubled his efforts, the increasingly heavy rain already soaking his clothes. My curiosity piqued, I ventured out of the shelter of our tree to get a better look at the proceedings.

Instead of a tug-o-war team, now that I was closer to the gate and could see the other speak, I could see something entirely unexpected. There were only the two men there, but the previously unseen fellow was arm-pit deep in a foul-looking pool of muddy water, or more accurately perhaps, given how it seemed to be resisting the first chap's attempts to extricate his friend, watery mud.

The man I'd seen first had found a long branch, which he had held out to the sinking chap, who had grabbed it, literally, for dear life. The rescuer gave another great heave and the man rose up out of the mud a little with a hideous squelching, sucking sound. I rushed to help but before I could join in, another almighty pull saw the man pop up out of the grasping sludge like a cork from a bottle. His rescuer fell over backwards with the sudden release and the two floundered on the bank, gasping for breath.

"I say," I said. "Are you two alright?"

The rescuer looked at me, panting. "Aye, thank you. Could have done with you a bit sooner though."

"Sorry about that, we didn't realise what was happening. We could only see you, so we assumed that you were pulling against someone else, not pulling one person up."

The mud-covered rescuee, catching his breath, smiled. "No harm done. They should really put up a warning sign about that pit though. Looked just like a patch of mud until I was in it up to my eyeballs."

Finally G. and B. realised what was going on and hurried over. It turned out that the bedraggled fellow had a car, and he took himself off home for a hot bath and a cup of tea. His rescuer, a farmer, thanked us for the belated offer of help, and headed on his way, whistling cheerfully.

My companions and I returned to stand beneath our tree to wait out the rain, which the farmer had assured us would not last long. We stood in thoughtful silence, listening to the hushed singing of birds, and the rustle and patter of the rain on the leaves above us, the tarmac of the road and on the grassy fields around us. I breathed in deeply, taking in the scents of soil and growing grass. Even Monty seemed content to sit at G.'s feet and enjoy the silence. We were sufficiently far off the main roads that at that moment we could not hear a single engine, and it was absolute bliss.

I closed my eyes, taking in the sounds and smells, when my simple enjoyment was ruined by a grunt. I opened my eyes and looked at G., from whom the noise had escaped.

"Yes, G. old thing?"

He looked at me in surprise. "Hmm? What's that?"

"You're thinking again aren't you?"

"Oh, well yes, but only a little."

"I should have known! Based on recent events, either this moment was going to be spoiled by some lunatic who doesn't believe in trousers, or who wants to outlaw trees or something, or you were going to start thinking."

"I'm terribly sorry J., you pay no attention to me. I doubt you'd understand anyway. You go back to what you were doing."

I didn't like the sound of that at all! Here he was, this fellow who called himself my friend, thinking thoughts and then keeping them all to himself. What selfish, self-centred greed! I was having none of it. "Oh I wouldn't would I? I wouldn't understand? You're thoughts are too high and lofty for the likes of intellectual midgets such as myself, is that it?"

"Not at all, I just…"

"You just nothing of the kind! Out with it then! Let's hear it!"

"I don't think that…"

"No, we want to hear it, don't we B.?"

B. blinked at me. "Pardon? Hear what?"

"You see!" I snapped. "We insist."

G. sighed. "Very well then. I was just thinking about the Devil."

It was my turn to blink. "Oh. What about him?"

"Well I was thinking again about the idea of evolution and sin, and about what that fellow was saying about good and evil and so on, and that got me on to thinking about the Devil."

"I see…" I said, nodding knowledgably.

"It's just that if sin is really just us acting upon those natural instincts with which we have arrived at in this phase of our evolution, then where does that leave old Lucifer?"

"Hmm… good point. Where does it leave him?"

"As I understand it, it was, or perhaps I should say is, Satan's job to tempt people and cause them to sin, thus disobeying the Will of God. If, however, it's simply primeval psychology that makes people want to disobey that Will, indeed it's the 'natural' state of a human being to wish to disobey, then that leaves the Devil rather out in the cold."

"It has been said," I pointed out cautiously, "that the greatest trick the Devil ever pulled was to convince people that he doesn't exist."

"Yes, that is true. But what if that chap was right about good and evil? What if there isn't such a thing as evil? Every human mind and soul is a battleground, a rope being pulled between opposing powers, but I suggest that rather than good and evil per se, the tug-o-war is between good, as revealed to us by God, and bestial instinct which is only evil in so far as it is merely lacking in goodness."

"So the battle isn't between God and Satan, but between God and Man?"

G. thought about that for a second. "No, not exactly. I think it would be better to say that it is a battle between what we were born to be, and what we were made to be, or possibly a battle between what we are, and what we could be. We have thus successfully replaced Satan with a scientific theory."

"I imagine that's more-or-less what a lot of fundamentalists think as well," I pointed out to him with a grin. "Can I add, though, that since he has no knowledge of God or His wishes, and thus acts solely according to instinct, Monty is a genuine and verifiable hell-hound, just as I have always affirmed." G. glared at me, but any reply was forestalled by the familiar smell of hot metal as B.'s mind ground into motion.

"That reminds me," B. said with a frown, "I think I understand all of that, but what about Hell then? If you're saying that the Devil doesn't exist, then presumably you're saying that Hell doesn't exist either?"

"I suppose not."

I nodded. "I've never been sure about Hell to be honest," I said. "It's always seemed a bit at odds with the rest of it."

"But doesn't the Bible talk about things being thrown into the fire? Chavs and so forth?"

"Yes, it does," I admitted, "but it's chaff, B. old thing, not chavs. Although if you throw chaff or dead wood or fruitless trees or any other metaphorical fuel into a fire, then that fuel is destroyed. The flame reduces it down to its component parts, and releases the energy that was stored therein when the thing was being made. Off it goes back into the carbon cycle or the nitrogen cycle or the water cycle or any other circular chemical thingy you care to mention. If you throw dry grass or wood on a fire, it doesn't stay in the flames being burnt constantly forever. If it did then the world would be covered in bonfires by now."

My friends nodded in understanding. "That's quite well put actually," G. said. I resented the implied surprise in his words, but decided not to make too much of it, this time. I had no doubt that the opportunity for revenge would present itself at some point. "So you'd go as far as destruction, but not permanent punishment?"

"Yes, I think so."

"Huh. Well that makes sense I suppose, although to my mind it seems a bit too much like playing semantics with metaphors."

"I think there are laws against that sort of thing," B. agreed, "although I'll vouch for the fact that J. has nothing against Jewish people at all, have you J.?"

"Certainly not, B. Now, it looks like it's stopped raining, so I think we'd better press on. We've still got a way to go before the next B&B."

Shouldering our packs once more, we sighed and stepped back out onto the road, leaving the birds far better educated than when we'd arrived.

Chapter 28

On faith and works.

The brief shower had cooled the air delightfully, but now as the sun reasserted itself and the moisture began to evaporate, it became frightfully muggy. The three of us began to sweat profusely, and Monty's tongue lolled out of his mouth as he trotted along ahead of us, ignorant of morality and a veritable black hole from the surface of which good could not escape.

I glanced across at my two friends, and saw that they were just as bad as me, red-faced and perspiring. Poor old B. was puffing like a bellows, the moisture pouring down his face like a ruddy Niagara Falls.

"I say you fellows," I gasped, "how about a breather?"

Without speaking, my companions staggered to the verge and collapsed down onto the now almost-dry grass. I fumbled around in my backpack and found my water bottle, which I found to contain about an inch of tepid fluid. I drank this and sighed.

I was about to dig out my map when we all heard the sound of hooves and rumble of wheels. Now the sight of a horse and carriage, even on the quiet country roads on which we travelled was sufficiently rare that we all stood to try and glimpse it. The carriage rounded a corner ahead of us, drawn by a single fine-looking beast. However, something wasn't quite right, and it took me a few seconds to figure out what it was. When I realised, I felt rather stupid, for the horse was behind the carriage, pushing it rather than pulling it in the usual fashion.

We waited as the carriage trundled up to us, and the fellow sitting on top gave us a cheery wave and turned to twitch the reins and bring his animal to a halt. Monty glowered up at the horse, as though trying to decide if it was worth his while in challenging. The horse bared its teeth at the little mutt, and Monty decided that it was beneath his notice after all.

"Hello there!" the driver said with a grin. "How do you do?"

"Very well, thank you," I replied. "And yourself?"

"Oh so-so. Could be better, could be worse. I'm in dire need of work really."

"Oh yes? You give people rides I imagine? Or do you do weddings and things like that?"

"Sometimes, yes."

"You're not a Hansom cab then?"

"Actually, I travel around the country giving acting lessons to people who wish to join the theatre."

"Ah," said B. "I see! You're a Stage Coach."

We all glared at him. Even Monty growled disapprovingly. In the silence that followed, I cannot swear that some tumble-weed blew past, but nor can I swear that it didn't. After a moment, I sighed and decided to change the subject. "So... this is a fine beastie that you have here. What's its name?"

"Her," he corrected. "Her name is Faith."

I stroked her nose, and she gave me an approving look. I

glanced at the carriage, which seemed rather a substantial one for a single animal to be hauling along, although she'd not seemed to be having problems when we first saw her.

"I see that you, ah, have gone with an unorthodox way of harnessing your horse," I said.

He smiled. "Yes, I know it seems rather odd this way round, but it really is much more satisfactory this way round than the other."

"Does she not," I asked, "become exhausted by pushing the coach like this? Especially by herself."

"Oh no, not at all. My old horse, also called Faith, had a severe problem with it, but that Faith was weak and fragile compared to the one I have now. No, the old Faith simply couldn't produce the work. My new Faith though is sufficiently strong that good work simply flows from her as a natural consequence."

G. frowned. "I'm sorry, I know you must hear this an awful lot, but are you not putting the cart before the horse here?"

He frowned. "You mean you think that the cart should push the horse? I wouldn't move at all if I tried doing that now would I? Anyway, I must be off. Good day!" And with that, he turned in his seat and flicked the reins. The horse set herself against the harness and began pushing the coach along.

We stared after him, scratching our heads. G. glanced at myself and B. "That did seem back to front to you as well didn't it?"

I thought about it for a while before replying. "I know that it *sounded* back to front, but I'm not actually certain that he wasn't right. In fact, I think given enough thought, I might actually prefer it his way around."

"And presumably," B. pointed out, "fewer horses are hurt in collisions that way. Oncoming traffic would hit the cart, not the animal. Much more humane."

"That is... also true," G. conceded.

We stood in silence for a bit, and then silently agreed to continue, turning our feet once more in the direction of Canterbury.

Chapter 29

On the belief in the divinity, or otherwise, of Christ.

For that night, we had booked a spot in a local campsite. We had been expecting the usual field, complete with toilet facilities that would have been considered minimal by those chaps who lived on top of pillars and ate locusts, and thought unsanitary by medieval Londoners. Instead, while it did indeed have a certain fieldiness to it, it also came with what at first sight appeared to be a large shed.

Closer inspection, however, revealed it to be an extremely cosy little building complete with a fireplace and wooden benches, in which weary campers could sit in warmth and comparative comfort until called into the loving embrace of their sleeping bags. A stack of firewood was neatly piled in one corner ready for use along with a pile of old newspapers for kindling, and a tap and concrete sink were provided for washing up. A most agreeable setup and one that I recommend to any and all campsite owners who might be reading this little work as worth their while installing on their property. A real five-star field this!

Having pitched tents and paid the owner the night's rent, we ensconced ourselves in this homely little hut. B. broke out a few cans of the best, and G. set to lighting the fire with a box of matches newly purchased from the last village. No messing around with fire-enablers or whatnot for us!

G. then set some sausages going and we sat around enjoying the warmth and light of the fire, eagerly anticipating the evening's repast. Indeed, our stomachs starting to grumble and gurgle so loudly that it seemed as though they were communicating, singing whale-like to each other in the quiet of the gathering dusk, mingling in a pre-digestive symphony of, I must frankly admit, little beauty or wonder.

B.'s abdomen gave a great baritone growl of such volume and magnitude that Monty was quite startled, turning to face what he knew could only be some giant grizzly bear come to fiendishly make off with the sausages that he was planning to rightfully steal. My readers may have gleaned from these pages that I do not hold little Montgomery in especially high regard, but even I was forced to admire his courage. He is not a large dog, although he is not one of those ghastly rat-on-a-string types that you see so many of nowadays, and was certainly not a young dog at the time of writing, having grown old in sin as it were. Nonetheless, here he was quite ready to fight to the last, with his back to the wall and believing firmly in the deliciousness of his cause.

B.'s stomach gave another reverberating rumble, and Monty lowered his head, baring his teeth and giving an answering growl. At this moment, my digestive tract chose to emit a sonorous snarl of its own and Monty spun to face this new menace, with teeth bared and ears flattened.

"Hey now Monty," G. cooed at him. "What's up with my little chap?" He bent down to pick up the wretched mongrel when his own stomach issued forth a leonine roar of anticipatory hunger. Monty gave a yelp and leapt backwards, staring with all the hurt of betrayed trust at the one human he had thought he could count on to watch the sausages while he fought off the hordes of untrammelled nature. At this exact moment, both B.'s stomach and my own joined in a most harmonious pre-digestive chord, and feeling himself to be surrounded by invisible beasts of considerable size, Monty took the better part and fled for the door, whimpering in terror.

He disappeared into the darkening night, and had been gone for less than a second when there was a cry, swiftly followed by a heavy thud, a loud 'oof!' sort of noise and a Montyesque yelp. We exchanged mildly concerned glances. I was concerned for whoever it was that had just fallen over the dog. G. was concerned for the dog. B. may have been concerned for both, or only that whatever it was that had just occurred might delay the serving of sausages. We shall never know.

There was a slight grunt from outside, and then a man entered, revealing the slightest trace of a limp. He looked at us and smiled. "Ah, hello. That your dog?"

"No," I said at exactly the same time as G. said 'Yes'. We glared at each other, and then both smiled at our guest. Not that he was a guest as such, since it wasn't really our barn, but we were there first so it felt more like ours than his if you know what I mean.

"Do sit down," I said warmly. "Beer?"

He did so gratefully, definitely favouring one leg over the other if I'm any judge of such things, and as the innocent victim of numerous Monty-related trippings, I feel that I am. "Did you say beer? Please then. I'm a little short of supplies myself."

I saw a look of anguish flit briefly across B.'s face, but he hid it well, with only a swift, wistful glance at the pile of sizzling sausages that was so very close to readiness.

G. passed him a beer, which he took politely, and took a deep draught with every sign of considerable enjoyment. The three of us followed suit. We introduced ourselves, and he nodded and smiled.

"My name's Morris Wild. So, you're hikers are you?"

"Um, sort of," I replied. It was a strange thing but despite being fully convinced of the sense, nay perhaps even the necessity of what my friends and I were about, it was still a little embarrassing to actually admit it to someone. "We're walking to Canterbury," I said, hoping that this would give him the gist without having to admit to a person of this rational twenty-first century that we were pilgrimaging.

He nodded. "Decent weather for it at least. Why Canterbury?"

"It seemed like a good idea at the time. Very Chaucerian, you know?"

He nodded again, and said something in a foreign language. I nodded knowledgeably and gave a small laugh to show that I knew exactly what he meant. He looked at me expectantly, and I realised he was waiting for an answer.

"Oh, yes," I said in as neutral a tone as possible. He seemed surprised and slightly puzzled but changed the subject of conversation. G. told me later that he had been speaking English à la Chaucer, and had asked me if I'd been sneaking into the beds of any millers' wives. Deuced impertinent question if you ask me!

World-weary as we were, we carefully kept the conversation on gentle and mundane things like politics and the Marmite question, eager to avoid giving the chap any opening to prove to us that he was another of the horde of madmen strewn into our path. On these subjects, he proved a knowledgeable and pleasant conversationalist, and we considered ourselves fortunate to have met such an erudite and charming fellow as Mr Wild.

The conversation turned to our journey and some of the curious people we had met upon our way. I don't know how it happened. I blame B., in the absence of solid evidence pointing towards anybody else. It is a policy that has stood me in good stead throughout my university career and beyond, and I have yet to see anything to make me doubt it.

We mentioned a few of those quaint individuals, and he seemed much amused by our tales of them, but then the name of Dick Dorking came up, and Mr Wild recoiled visibly, for a moment a look of distaste and dislike clouding that placid physiognomy.

"Ah!" he cried mopping his brow with a handkerchief. "Please do not mention That Name in my presence! Unfortunate souls, that you had to meet That Man on your travels!"

"You are not then," I enquired, "a proponent of Mr D... of the person in question's theories of amolecularism?" Even the name of the theory was enough to make Mr Wild shudder.

"Ugh! No, my goodness gracious, no! Repellent man, ridiculous school of thought! A blight sirs, a blight upon the earth!"

I nodded. "I'm very glad to say that we are all in agreement with you, although possibly not to the same extent."

"Only because of your lack of exposure to the vile man's ludicrous imaginings!"

"Well quite," G. said, "what sort of idiot can look at the world in a scientific age and doubt the existence of molecules?"

"Ah, well of course I think it is only reasonable for intelligent and educated people to doubt the literal interpretation of the theory," Wild replied, "but that doesn't mean that we have to abandon the theory altogether does it?"

G.'s brows knitted. "I beg your pardon? You don't hold to a literal interpretation of molecular theory?"

"But of course not!" Wild said with astonishment. "Naturally I believe in atoms, one must you know, in this time and culture, but to talk of them joining together as molecules? That is a very different kettle of fish! Much less plausible if you ask me."

"You believe in atoms, but not molecules?" I asked, scratching my head.

"I think that it is highly important to believe in atoms, although even then I think that their importance is far more symbolic than necessarily factual. It so improves people when they believe in symbolic artefacts such as atoms, and even molecules, as long as we accept that they are merely symbolic of something else utterly."

"Such as?"

"Ah, well of course that depends on the cultural and temporal lens through which they are viewed. The same symbol can have wildly different meanings across cultures and times you see."

"And while you do believe, to some extent at least, in atoms, you consider molecules to be entirely non-existent?" G. asked.

"If you must put it is such definite terms, then I suppose so, sort of."

"What absolute rot!" B. exclaimed. "What's the point of believing in atoms if you don't believe in molecules? Now

I'm no great scientific genius," he glared at G. and myself, daring us to agree, "but surely if atoms don't form molecules, how are they supposed to do anything?"

"Atoms can react quite well with each other," Wild replied, "without needing to take on a new and mingled, co-joined form to do it."

"But all of the interactions between elements lead to the creation of molecules," G. pointed out. "And the interactions between molecules and elements, and between molecules and other molecules are far more numerous, more varied and more wonderful than anything that occurs solely between elements."

"I see," he said with a sad shake of his head, "that you are stuck in the molecular fundamentalism of yesteryear, when a literal interpretation of the molecular doctrine satisfied the unthinking and uneducated layman. I am saddened my friends, saddened."

"But how," I asked, "can you castigate Dorking the way you have, and then tell us that you yourself do not believe in molecules? Surely that makes you an amolecularist as well doesn't it?"

"Certainly not!" he cried. "I acknowledge the crucial symbolic importance of molecular theory in day-to-day life, and how important it is that we maintain our faith in atoms while remaining aware on an intellectual level that it is all merely symbolic."

"Then the whole thing just falls down!" I said, getting a little heated. "There's absolutely no point believing in atoms without believing in molecules, because if the atoms are unable to react and form molecules, then they don't do anything at all. If you take that view, you may as well just give up and admit that you're one of Dorking's amolecularists after all and save yourself some time and everybody else a lot of confusion."

"But I still live my life in accordance with a molecularist viewpoint!"

"But why?"

"Because... well, um... because the metaphors are important. They have deeper meanings."

"I think it would be morally and intellectually far more honest to simply say 'I don't believe in that really' and act accordingly," G. said with a sniff.

"Hang on though," I said. "I think I can see the point of behaving as though you believed in something even though you don't because you think that it is a better way of living."

"You see," Wild said smugly. "At least someone here knows what I mean."

"Now hang on! I didn't say that I agreed with you. As far as I can tell, you're saying that you don't believe in the actuality of molecules and things, but that they're just metaphors for... what?"

"Oh, well. You know. Metaphors for... life and so on. All very metaphorical. And look here, it still makes perfect logical sense to believe in molecules. It's a perfectly rational viewpoint to take, as long as you understand that it's not really true."

"Yes... I see. I'm sorry, but you seem to want to have your cake and eat it. Either way that I suggest has what G. refers to as 'moral honesty'. What you want to do is say you sort of believe it, except that you don't, but still live as though it weren't not untrue. Um, I think. But as it is, you can't say that it's sort of true-ish and adopt that smug air of intellectual superiority over us by dint of avoiding definite beliefs. You might very well be right for all I know. Perhaps molecules are just metaphorical. But if that's the case, then the sugar you put in your metaphorical tea will be metaphorical as well, and my real tea will be all the sweeter."

Chapter 30

On the idea that religion is merely a prop for the morally and intellectually weak.

We went to bed soon after the conversation with Mr Wild, and I spent another cheerless night under canvas (or whatever marvellous space-age flame-retardant, heat-expelling, spider-attracting, rock-and-hummock-seeking material modern tents are made of).

The next morning dawned bright and a touch chilly, and we made a swift breakfast and pressed on our way. Our time off from the travails of modern life was finite, and we had yet to reach Canterbury, although we were drawing ever nearer.

As the morning progressed, the sun dispelled the early chill and the temperature climbed steadily. We passed through quiet country roads and little hamlets of the most picturesque and bucolically quaint sort, and made good time. The birds were singing, the bees buzzed lazily about their business, and even B. hadn't complained about his feet for almost twenty-five minutes.

We passed through another of these lovely, albeit somewhat remote, little settlements, and out through the other side. About five minutes afterwards, we passed an incredibly old woman heading in the opposite direction. I am not attempting to be rude when I describe her as such. She looked quite capable of reminiscing about the war in Europe and the eventually downfall of that hated dictator Napoleon Bonaparte, and of complaining about the introduction of the Spinning Jenny. She was small, shrivelled and hunched, and leaned heavily on a walking frame which she shuffled forwards between each step, achieving a maximum velocity of almost an eighth of a mile an hour. As she approached (or more accurately perhaps, as we approached her) she peered at us through magnifying-glass spectacles and smiled.

"Good morning," she said in a high, quavering voice.

Being a well-brought-up sort of a chap, I tipped my hat to her. "And a very good morning to you too ma'am."

"I'm just going to the shop," she said, as though she felt the need to explain why she was tottering along this isolated country road by herself.

"Ah," I said, smiling. G. and B. gave her their most charming and polite smiles, and even Monty didn't growl and bare his teeth at her, which for him is the height of polite respect.

"Isn't it a wonderful day?" she trembled, beaming up at the sky and the trees.

It is a theory of mine, borne up by considerable experience, that the older one gets, the more one becomes more so. That is, the more like yourself you get. If one is a snappish, slightly bitter sort of person at heart, then as one gets older it comes out more and more, and you stop saying please and thank you and start acting as though it's all everybody else's fault. On the other hand, if one is of a fundamentally relaxed and benevolent disposition to start with, then as you get older, the more condensed this state becomes. In the same way an apple, if left to dry, shrinks and becomes wrinkled, but it also grows sweeter as there is less water to dilute the natural sugars already present.

This little old lady was definitely of the latter breed, a shrivelled old apple bursting with natural sweetness, and I found myself warming to her greatly.

"It is indeed," I enthused. "Have you had far to walk?"

"Oh no," she said, still beaming, "only a half mile or so. But I'm not so quick as I was. I'm quite old you know." She gave a shy, conspiratorial smile as she said this, as though it were a great secret.

"Surely not!" I cried, all gallantry. "Why, you can't be a year over thirty-five!" My friends nodded their agreement.

"Forty, tops," G. murmured.

She beamed at us. "Such polite young men," I wasn't certain if she was complimenting us, or commenting to herself.

"We really mustn't keep you," I said, tipping my hat again. "Good day."

"Good day to you, too." She gave us another beaming smile, before turning back to her walking frame with an expression of utmost concentration. She shuffled it forwards perhaps three inches, and took a couple of steps up to it, paused for a couple of seconds' rest and then shuffled the frame forwards another three inches. She seemed perfectly happy, and the weather promised to continue fine, so the three of us (and Monty of course) continued on our way.

After what I assume was about half a mile, we passed the wrought-iron gates of what I at first took to be a very large house, but then my eye caught a large sign. 'Knackers Yard Care Home' it proclaimed in large, curling script. Through one of the windows, I could see a pair of old men hunched over a game board of some sort, and in the yard in front of the house I could see a couple of elderly persons enjoying the sunshine under the watchful gaze of a nurse. This then must have been the start point of our recent acquaintance.

We passed on by and kept going for another ten minutes or so when we overtook an old man shuffling along in the same direction as us.

"Good morning," I said cheerily as I passed him.

"Huh," he grunted, peering up at the sky suspiciously. "What's good about it? I'll get sun-burnt for sure."

A sour apple this one then! Nonetheless, I was determined to be friendly. "You've just come from the old people's home?"

"Huh. Prison more like. Place to cram you while they're waiting for you to die. Vultures!"

"Yes, well. If that's how you want to look at it."

"We've just met one of your fellows," B. said, also trying to lighten this old codger's mood. "A little old lady."

The chap turned to glare at him. "Hah! Small and shrivelled, like a rotten prune?"

B. frowned. "I'm not sure that's really very..."

"Has to use one of those ridiculous walking frames?"

"It seemed very helpful."

"Hah! Only if you need one. I don't!" he proclaimed, thumping himself heartily on the chest. This caused a violent coughing fit, and I was just wondering whether he'd swallowed his dentures and if any of us knew the Heimlich manoeuvre when it cleared and he straightened up again, glaring at us defiantly.

"Nope, no walking frame for me! I don't even need a walking stick! Not even on wet days."

"Good for you," I said without much feeling. "I think we'd better be getting..."

"Because I'm not weak, see? I can stand on my own two feet! I don't need anything propping me up to make my way in the world. I get on just fine under my own steam thank you very much! It's only the weak and feeble, like the prune-woman who need that kind of support. Not capable of holding themselves up without their sticks and frames and whatnots to lean on! No excuse for being feeble, no matter your age. Look at me now, ninety-six years old and still quite capable of walking to the village shop for my own baccy. Not many can say that at my age!"

I paused, puzzled. "I see, well you really must be very strong and all as you say. Travelling under your own steam and so forth."

He raised his chin defiantly. "That's right!"

"Only," I said after a moment, "isn't the village back that way?"

He stared at me for a second, and then looked down the road in the direction he'd been travelling, and back again the way he'd come. He looked back at me with a ferocious glare, as though it were my fault.

"It seems to me," I said sternly, "that it's all very well calling that nice old lady weak and feeble and all the rest, but at least she's travelling in the right direction!"

We left the bitter old chap opening and closing his mouth as he searched in vain for a suitable reply. When I looked back a minute or so later, he had turned around and was shuffling back towards the old people's home, shoulders slumped.

Chapter 31

The 'invention' of God.

We had left the old people's home and it's varyingly pleasant inhabitants some way behind and were once more making good time. We were hiking along, talking of inconsequential things when a cloud passed in front of the sun.

I tutted to myself and waited for it to pass, but instead the shadow that we had been plunged into deepened. I wondered if we might not be in for a rain storm seeing how dark it was getting, but upon looking around, I realised that all around us was bright sunshine still. I wondered if we were the victim of a cartoonish cloud hovering directly overhead. Then I realised two things. Firstly, the shadow around us was growing. Secondly, 'us' was no longer accurate because G. and B. had dived into the ditch beside the road, and Monty was nowhere to be seen.

"Look out J. you imbecile!" G. yelled.

I turned and looked up to see the sky falling on me. I let out a terrified yelp and performed a dive my old PE teacher would have been proud of, moving from the road to the ditch with a single prodigious leap, without a run-up or anything. I hit the bottom of the ditch and rolled in the muddy, brackish water at the bottom as a vast red *thing* roared overhead. I saw a flicker of flame and one thought passed through my head. "By Jupiter's beard!" I murmured in horror. "*Dragons!*"

I mourned for the gentle, modern Britain, devoid of heroes to combat the winged, fire-breathing beasts that would soon lay waste our green and pleasant land. Then I reflected on the quality of anti-aircraft fire and started worrying a little less.

"Quick!" I hissed to my companions. "We need to call in the RAF! They'll need to scramble a couple of fighters to deal with that monster! Let's hope they'll give us some sort of reward for spotting it. I might even have the head mounted on my wall..." I pictured myself posing beside the slain animal, dangling from some sort of crane perhaps.

I further imagined myself in my hunting room (I would need to get a hunting room), showing off the head and saying very modestly, "And here's a little something I bagged over the fields of Kent. Now come and see the stuffed dinosaur. Running loose through the villages of England don'tcherknow?"

G. gave me a look of mixed scorn and (very) mild concern. "I think you might have hit *your* head J. You're blithering. More so that is."

"What? You saw that monster!" I paused. "Didn't you?" I rallied myself. "If you didn't see that dragon bearing down on us, why are you in the ditch eh?" I asked triumphantly.

"What on earth are you talking about?" he asked wearily, climbing up out of the ditch.

"I say," B. said, "I think he came down just over that hedge. Shouldn't we go and make sure that he's alright?"

"Alright?" I cried, scarcely able to believe what I was hearing. "Do you want to be eaten, B.? He'll snap you up as soon as you go near him!"

"I think, B.," G. said, "that J. must have hit his head

jumping into the ditch, and has got a touch of the concussion. I think it best if we just ignore whatever he says from this point on."

"Well if it wasn't a dragon, what on earth was it?" I asked, crossing my arms. "It was huge and red and breathing fire. Dragon."

"It was a hot air balloon you dolt! It's just crashed down over there, and we're going to go and see if everyone's okay."

"Oh." Now that I came to think about it, jumping to a draconic conclusion did seem like a bit of a small step for man, but a giant leap for logic. "Yes, a hot air balloon. That would of course have been my second guess."

"Of course," G. nodded. I turned away, but still saw him look at B. and circle his finger around his temple and nod in my direction. Well let them think what they may, but when the pines go up like torches, and fiery death comes sweeping out of the night sky on vast and ancient wings, to burn and consume the lands of men, I hope they don't come running to me!

We hurried over to a gate through the hedge and clambered over it. Once over, we could see the crashed balloon. The balloon bit of it was almost completely deflated, and all we could make out of the basket was a large, squarish lump in the middle of a mass of red material. Monty paused and growled at it, and for the tiniest moment I felt a kind of kindred with the little mongrel. He also clearly saw the dragonishness of it. Then the moment passed and I saw Monty once again for the diabolical third-of-a-Cerberus that he really was.

We rushed over to the collapsed balloon and started trying to haul the material out of the way so that we could get at the basket. Hot air balloons look very stately and impressive when bobbing about up in the atmosphere, but when there's less hot air then there seems to be an awful lot more balloon.

I could hear muffled shouting from somewhere beneath the sea of scarlet nylon, and I could see some sort of movement from the top of the square shape of the concealed basket. There was a sudden thud and the deadened sound of someone saying something along the lines of 'whoooof!' I tugged at part of the balloon when suddenly a face appeared before me.

The face belonged to a portly old man, possessed of a magnificent pair of moustaches and an equally magnificent pair of jowls. He had wire-rimmed spectacles that were now considerably askew, and his white hair was up in a series of violent tufts.

"Aha!" he cried as he saw me. "Freedom! Returned from the belly of the beast, what?"

He struggled a little, and with my help, a short, stocky body appeared, clad in a tweed suit. He stood and straightened his glasses. He beamed at the three of us cheerfully, then turned a severe glance on the crashed balloon and tutted.

"Bad luck! Rotten bad luck," he muttered. "But there you are, what goes up and so on eh?"

"I say, are you alright?" I asked.

He turned to me with an expression of surprise. "Of course! Why on earth wouldn't I be?"

"You have just collided with a planet," G. pointed out. "People occasionally get damaged doing things like that."

"Bah!" He waved his hand dismissively. "I'm doing it all the time, and I've never been healthier!" He paused and stared at the flaccid, flopping balloon. He took a deep breath in, releasing it slowly. "Marvellous really isn't it? Quite wonderful. A most incredible invention. Shame it's all gone out though."

"Oh absolutely! I've never been up in one, but I've always fancied it. The world's first flying machines. And never fear, I'm sure you'll get it back in order again."

He frowned. "Eh? Not the balloon! I'm talking about the air."

"The air?"

"Yes. The air that was in my balloon, keeping it up."

G. looked puzzled. "I'm not sure that air was invented as such," he said, "I think it sort of developed by itself."

"Stuff and piffle!" the old chap snorted. "The French invented it in the late 18th century."

"No no, that was the balloon," G. said firmly. "The Montgolfier brothers made their first balloon in the late 18th century."

"Of course they did! But it wasn't much use really was it, with no air to fill it with!"

"Of course there was air! Otherwise everyone would have suffocated!"

"Nonsense! Air is made up of nitrogen and carbon dioxide and oxygen and that sort of thing, what? No mention of them until the 19th century. They had something called phlogiston before that."

"No, you've got it wrong. Phlogiston wasn't real. They were mistaken. They were thinking about oxygen, but it hadn't been discovered yet."

"So oxygen wasn't around before that then?"

"Of course it was! It just hadn't been discovered!"

The chap looked at G. with an expression of mingled scorn and pity. It was sort of like the expression I used on Monty, except that mine had no pity in it.

"My dear fellow, the stuff would have been everywhere! Had it been there, people would have tripped over it straight away. I'm sorry but logic and common sense dictate that air did not come into existence until people required it to fill hot air balloons with."

"But surely they wouldn't have invented hot air balloons in the first place if they didn't already have air to heat and put in balloons!" G. was becoming heated now.

"Of course not! They invented hot air balloons, and then realised that they wouldn't work until they had something to fill the balloon with, so they set to work inventing something."

"Well why didn't they just fill it with phlogiston?" G. asked, dripping sarcasm like a bloodhound's drool.

"Because it didn't work!" The old fellow was getting annoyed now as well. "You may as well ask why we shouldn't fill combustion engines with water!"

"But it doesn't make any sense! You wouldn't develop something like the hot air balloon without first perceiving that hot air rises. Otherwise why would you have the idea of putting it in a balloon? It doesn't make any sense I say!"

"Well thank you for coming and making sure I'm alright," the balloonist said, his face growing dark, "but don't let me keep you."

We took the hint and left. "Don't worry yourself, G." I said reassuringly as we crossed back across the field. "There's not much phlogiston up there. It's probably affected his brain."

B. was about to add a reassurance of his own, but gave a yelp instead, his feet flew out from under him and he crashed to the turf.

G. and I heaved him up between us. "Steady on their

fellow," I said. "Thanks to chaos theory, you've most likely just caused an earthquake in the eastern hemisphere."

"The eastern hemisphere?" G. asked with raised eyebrows. "Given the size of him, I'm surprised we're not experiencing a ten-Richter right here!"

B. gave him a death-ray glare. "I am not fat! I just have a lot of gravitas!" He turned to glare at the ground where he'd slipped. "And I wouldn't have fallen at all if someone hadn't left their rubbish lying around in the middle of nowhere!" He stooped and picked up a round, shiny object. "Look, someone's gone and dumped their broken old pocket-watch in the middle of a field!"

"Maybe someone dropped it by accident?" I suggested.

"Don't you believe it! I bet it was done on purpose!" He threw it back down onto the ground, and we headed back to the road.

Chapter 32

The universe according to atheists.

Having left behind the wrecked balloon, and put its curious and confused owner behind us, we pressed on. We were within spitting distance of our goal now and I was starting to wish the whole thing was just over and done with. It's curious, but you can be the firmest of friends with a chap, but after several days of continuous close proximity, you find yourself heartily wishing that you could beat them to death with their own wretched squeaky walking boot, or possibly choke them on their own ratty little dog.

"I say, did you hear me, J.?"

I looked at B. "Hmmm? I beg your pardon old chap, what did you say? Lost in thought there."

"I said that my back hurts! Can't we stop? I think I've done myself a severe injury falling over that watch. I might have slipped a ligament, or got myself a spinning disc! I could keel over paralysed at any second. *And* my feet hurt!"

"I'm sure that you're just a little bruised," I said with infinite patience. Sometimes, I think that I should write to the Vatican and nominate myself for sainthood. Not very modest perhaps, but if I sent B. as my messenger, I'm sure that they would quickly come over to my way of thinking.

"Actually," G. cut in, "I think a stop would be good. I'm worried about little Monty."

I peered at the little mongrel. He gazed back with malevolent humour. "What on earth's wrong with 'little Monty'?

"It's his paws. He's not used to such long journeys, and these roads aren't exactly the best. What if he stepped on some broken glass?"

"I'm sure the glass would be fine."

G. chose to ignore this rapier riposte. "Perhaps I should have bought him a little pair of walking boots. You can get them in very small children's sizes you know."

"You'd have to get two pairs though," B. pointed out.

I tried to imagine Monty waddling along in two pairs of miniature walking boots. Insomuch as I can read his expression, Monty appeared to be doing much the same, and coming to a very similar conclusion. Then, as though in fear that this plan might be suddenly enacted, he bolted. Before any of us could do or say anything, he was galloping off far ahead.

"His paws seem alright to me," I remarked drily, eliciting a glare from G.

"Monty! Monty, come here!" he shouted. "Monty! Heel! Monty! Stay!" Monty did none of these things. Instead, he suddenly turned off the road through a gateway and disappeared from sight. We hiked up to where he'd vanished, and found ourselves staring up at a grand old house set in a large garden. The garden was generally well kept, although the lawns could perhaps have done with a bit of trim, and the flower beds had a few more weeds than might have been deemed proper for Cheltenham.

"There you are! Come here boy!" I looked up to see

Monty standing in the doorway of the house. The door was standing wide open, and Monty was peering inside, tail up in an inquisitive fashion. He looked round at the sound of G.'s voice, regarded him in a distinctly insolent manner, and then as though a decision had been made for him, turned back and trotted into the house.

I let out a little chuckle, partly in pleasure at the vindication of my opinions regarding 'little Monty', and partly in amusement at the expression of astonishment on G.'s face.

"I suppose we'd better go and find him..." G. said hesitantly.

I checked my watch. "No time. Sorry G, but the weak must fall by the wayside etc etc. We mourn his loss but the journey must continue and all that." I turned to go, but G. cleared his throat noisily.

"He might get hurt! We don't know what's in there!"

I considered this hopefully for a moment, but then something else occurred to me. "On the other hand, he might steal more underwear, and I don't want to be prosecuted as some sort of canine-enabled pervert, so I suppose we'd better find him."

"They might have seats in there," B. said wistfully. "Maybe even... armchairs..." His eyes misted up.

Thus decided, we approached the house. There was a doorbell, and I was about to press it when I looked through the open door and saw the utter barrenness within. There was no furniture, no ornaments, paintings, lampshades or fittings. Even the floor was bare boards. This house was obviously no longer in a state of occupation.

I stepped into the bare hallway. "Hello?" I called. It might look deserted, but you never know.

"Hello! We're looking for my dog," G. shouted from behind me. "He's really quite harmless."

I stepped hesitantly inside, feeling extremely sheepish. It's odd that the concept of property has been ingrained so firmly into our psyches that stepping into someone else's house uninvited, even when the house is clearly abandoned, makes one feel so intensely uncomfortable, as though ants of outraged judgement are crawling over one's skin.

To alleviate this feeling somewhat, I called out several more times, but to no avail. The house was clearly empty. Looking through the rooms in search of Monty, but increasingly out of curiosity, and a growing sense of excitement at sneaking around somewhere we knew to be forbidden, we found empty rooms and bare floors. The wallpaper had been stripped, and the house could have been standing empty for weeks or hours; it was impossible to say.

We had begun to relax, and the ants-of-judgement feeling had now completely passed. There was however, no sign of Monty, and we had now searched the entire ground floor.

"I suppose we'd better look upstairs then?" I asked. G. nodded and we headed for the stairs. As I placed my foot on the lowest stair though, a bell started ringing, and I almost jumped out of my skin. The bell was replied to with a surprised yapping. I paused, and realised that what I could hear was a clock striking the hour somewhere above us. I frowned at the other two, who looked similarly surprised. We had seen not a stick of furniture in the entire place. Why on earth would there be a clock upstairs?

Suddenly tentative once more, we ascended the stairs. We could hear growling from a room down the landing, and it was in this direction that we went. I stuck my head round the doorpost (the door being absent) and found myself looking into a large room. It was, like the rest of the house, denuded of carpets and wallpaper. However, unlike the rest of the house, it did have a lone piece of furniture, and what a piece!

We entered the room and stared in awe at a grandfather clock, almost tall enough to reach the ceiling. If Da Vinci, Stradivarius, Robert Stephenson and Chippendale had all somehow got together and said, 'As a team-building exercise, let's make a really amazing clock!' they could not have come up with something better than this. Aesthetically, it was beautiful. The wood had a deep reddish lustre, and the varnish was undisturbed by crack or chip. The glass of the face was flawless, the face itself a work of art. Furthermore, working on the fact that my watch was two minutes fast, G's was thirty seconds slow, and B's thirty-seven minutes and twelve seconds slow, we calculated that it was showing exactly the right time, down to the split second. As we stared at it, it struck again, and it was as though choirs were singing choruses of heavenly music. I could have spent my entire life sitting in front of that clock and never grown bored. I would have grown hungry, and would probably then have left, but bored? Never!

Monty was standing in a pose of defiance, snarling at the aforementioned masterpiece. G. snatched him up. "Monty! What are you doing up here! Bad boy!"

I ignored the diminutive mutt, still examining the clock with rapt interest. "Why do you suppose they left it?" I asked.

B. shook his head. "I've no idea. Lovely old thing though isn't it?"

"I'll say! But it must be worth an absolute mint! Why would they leave this, out of everything in the house?"

B. shrugged. "Maybe it was too big to move."

"Or perhaps it came with the house," G. suggested,

somewhat doubtfully.

Gazing at that wonderful old clock, I was suddenly struck by a wave of utter melancholy. To see this gorgeous, amazing old clock, a masterpiece in every sense, abandoned in these dingy and uninhabited surroundings struck a chord in my heart.

"How beautiful, how wonderful, and how utterly pointless," I murmured.

G. looked at me with an odd expression on his face. "I beg your pardon?"

I gestured at the clock. "Don't you see? This intricate, beautiful, wonderful thing, and yet it might just as well not be here at all."

He and B. frowned. "I don't see why not," B said. "It's gorgeous old thing, and bang on the dot as well."

I shrugged. "So what? It doesn't matter if it's correct to the nanosecond, or twenty-three hours and fifty-nine seconds slow. There's no one here to see it, and thus it is as worthless as a stick in the garden. In fact, I think the stick is rather more useful. At least it will eventually rot and fertilise the flower bed."

"Don't be ridiculous," G. said. "It's doing exactly what it's meant to do. It's being beautiful, and it's telling the time."

"No, it's not."

"You don't consider it beautiful then?"

"Oh no, I think it's absolutely sublime. But beauty's in the eye of the beholder. Until we entered the house, it wasn't beautiful at all. It just was. And it wasn't telling the time, because there wasn't anyone for it to tell the time to."

"Of course it does!" G. replied, "The cogs are still turning, the hands are still moving. It's still displaying the time."

"But it's not! It's just turning and spinning and ticking,

and that's all. Parts are moving, but they're not moving anywhere. They're not moving to do anything, because what they're designed to do requires someone to do it to. A clock in and of itself has no concept of time. It doesn't tell the time, it just turns its parts in a regular and repeated manner. If no one is there to look at those parts and interpret them as indicating a time, then they're not doing anything at all. Not really."

B. scratched his head. "Is this one of those 'If there's one hand flapping in the forest, does it make two in the bush?' things? Because they always give me headaches."

"I'm just saying," I continued, "that it doesn't matter how massive and intricate and beautiful this clock is, it is completely pointless, and completely worthless. It doesn't do anything, it's not for anything. Why is it here at all?"

"But why should it have a point?" G. asked. "Why can't it just be?"

I thought for a moment. "It could just be, it's true," I conceded, "although I think that asking why it should have a point is as pointless a question as asking why it shouldn't." I paused for a moment more. "If you could have one of these clocks, would you keep it here, in this empty bedroom, or have it in the hallway at home, where it will brighten the house and give people perfect time day in and day out? It seems to me that if it's the former, you may as well not have it at all. If it's all the same to you, I would like my clock to not only keep perfect time, but to tell me what it is, too. You can keep yours turning around to itself in a locked and darkened room if you like. I'll have mine shining and ticking and spinning _for_ something, and mine will have been much better worth the price."

I started at a sound from downstairs. Just the creaking of a silent house, but it reminded me of our situation. "Now, let's grab Monty and get out of here before we're nabbed for trespass," I said. "At least he's not found any knickers to steal this time."

G. grabbed him up and we hurried back down to continue on our way, leaving that sad, solitary, sublime old clock ticking away in that empty old house by the road.

Chapter 33

On Free Will and the merits of choice as opposed to forced compliance.

We pressed onwards, leaving that melancholy old house behind us, and soon the balmy air and gentle breeze had quite restored my dampened spirits. B. was still muttering about his feet, but as far as I could tell it was more out of a desire for something with which to pass the time than out of any expectation of being listened to.

Another one of those picturesque but curiously identical small villages ambled slowly into view and allowed us to approach, passing between freshly painted bungalows with small but impeccably kept front gardens. The few shops and the pub that we passed had hanging baskets sprouting from them in every direction and the whole affair just begged to be sabotaged one night by the next village along. More than one civil war has been started by the glittering allure of the Best Kept Village cup. Indeed, the Wars of the Roses, as the name suggests, began over just such a dispute, and they resulted in the deaths of thousands and the whole country being laid to waste. County councillors take note! It may be a harmless competition to you, but to others it is the start of a century of rapine and slaughter!

Having passed beneath the Hanging Baskets of Babylon without even seeing fire or the sword, we reached the centre of the village and began the outward journey. Suddenly we heard a noise, and paused. It is strange how the sound of laughing children affects different people differently. It makes G. looked slightly anxious, as he tried to remember if he has fed the children, and let them in from the garden before it got dark. B. shudders slightly, hunches his shoulders and glowers at the ground. B. doesn't like children you see. For me, it brings Vietnam-esque flashbacks of hellish days in the playground, and the no-doubt innocent laughter of today's children becomes the mocking jeers of the youngsters of yesteryear as they attempt to break my spirit and crush my soul, but they shan't dash it all! They shan't! I'll tell teacher! I'll go and... yes, well. That's the effect it has on me. Horrid stuff, the old post-traumatic stress wotsit.

Anyhow, once G. has remembered that he had indeed let the children in, B. had shaken off his automatic defensiveness, and the two of them had pried my limbs from around the nearest lamp-post and calmed me down a bit, we looked for the source of the sound. People where I grew up were of the opinion that children should be seen (if absolutely necessary, briefly at Christmas for example) but not heard, and that goes twice if they're happy. The sound of children having fun drifting through the streets is one that is somewhat odd to me, and as such required a little investigation.

Happily, said investigation turned out to be on our way anyway, and as we plodded onwards the noise got louder. We presently came to a well-kept house with a reasonably-sized garden in front of it, surrounded by a painted wooden fence. The garden itself was awash with small people having what looked like considerable amounts of fun. Not being an expert at guess-the-age, I would estimate that they were somewhere around the four- or five-year mark, but since I couldn't get to examine the length of their teeth or lop off a limb to count the rings (or at least, not without being arrested by an unsympathetic police force) I can't give you an accurate figure.

"Children, it's time to come in now!" I looked up and saw a woman standing at the door of the house.

Some of the children closer to her looked up and glanced around at the others. Most appeared to have heard, and were staring wistfully at various toys and games that they had been busy with. A few of the more dutiful children left what they were doing and trooped towards the house. Others ignored the instruction, or pretended that they hadn't heard and carried on with their games, although a slightly surly, surreptitious note had entered their play.

We watched with leisurely interest, expecting the woman to start shouting. It is a terrible truth of the human condition that we do enjoy to see others exasperated. Not angry, or upset exactly. No one wants to see others hurt or irritated, but exasperated has a certain comedy of its own.

We were disappointed. She did not shout. She did not sigh or huff. She didn't even look so much as put out. She simply stood by the door with a patient smile on her face and waited. The recalcitrant children continued to ignore her, although a few looked up with apprehensive expressions, as though expecting wrathful retribution, and the more time that passed, the more apprehensive looks there were. One or two of the little tykes gave each other nervous glances, left their play and hurried inside, flinching slightly as they approached the door and the waiting woman. Instead of the expected tellings off though, she smiled kindly and ushered them through the door.

Some of the other children saw this. Some of those who saw appeared to relax a little as they realised that they weren't going to get in trouble for coming in late and hurried in after the others. Others though saw that they weren't being shouted at and just carried on playing.

We continued to watch for several minutes, and the woman continued to wait patiently, and the remaining children, the naughtiest ones I presume, continued to ignore her and play. The woman noticed us watching and moved across the garden towards us. We suddenly became aware that the situation was a little awkward. A little open to wilful misinterpretation if you see what I mean. Three strange men standing watching a group of children playing for several minutes. And men come no stranger than my two companions!

Happily, she didn't appear to be too cross, so we waited for her to approach, before bidding her a good day.

"Good day to you too," she said smiling.

"Are they all yours then?" I asked, gesturing vaguely in the direction of the small people.

"Oh no!" she laughed, "only two of them. But the oldest is having a birthday party, so all his classmates have come round."

"Ah, of course. Um... I'm not a parent, to my knowledge anyway, but I thought that you had to be a bit firmer with children."

She frowned, puzzled. "Some people are, yes. Why do you ask?"

"It's just that if my mother had told me to come inside, and I'd ignored her like some of those little rascals ignored you, I'd have received a hiding and a half! You seem quite content to let them do as they will."

She beamed at me. "You've got it!"

I hopped a hurried step back. "Oh, well they say it's not infectious anymore, and you can hardly see the..."

"Oh, no, I mean you understand the idea."

"Really? I do? Oh, yes, well of course I do! A very understanding sort of chap me."

"Except about innocent dogs..." G.'s voice muttered behind me.

"If I meet one, I'll let you know how it goes," I muttered back.

"The whole idea you see is to give the children absolute free choice about what they do and how they do it."

"Hang on, I just heard you tell them to all come in. That's not really letting them do things for themselves is it?"

"I told them what I wanted them to do, but I'm not making them do it. After all, there wouldn't be any value to their doing what they were asked if I forced them to would there?"

"I suppose not. I imagine it rather depends on why you're asking them to come inside."

"Oh, it's because it was time to blow the candles out on the cake. All the ones who've gone inside are having theirs now."

"Ah, so if the others had just done as they were told, they would even now be enjoying delicious cake?"

"That's right."

"But surely," G. said, "if you'd only told them to come in and have some cake, they would all have come?"

She considered this. "Yes, but then they would have been done as they were told out of expectation of reward, not because it was the right thing to do."

THOMAS JONES

"But how," G. persisted, "do they know that what you are telling them is the right thing to do? You could have been caning each child as they went through the door, and then sending them to bed without any supper."

"But why on earth would I do that? Why would I invite all of these innocents into my home, and let them play in the sunshine in the safety of my garden, where they can learn to play together and grow wiser and better suited for what is to come, and then suddenly and arbitrarily punish them?"

"But what about the children who didn't come in because they didn't know there was cake."

"At the very start of the party, I told the children that there was going to be a cake. Not long ago, I sent my son out to remind them. Now I've called them in, and if they are too busy getting on with whatever it is they are doing out here then that is their decision and I won't interfere with them."

"But," asked B., "will there not be some cake left for them when the other children have had theirs? Surely they'll still get some to take home with them?"

The woman smiled. "I suppose we'll have to wait and see, won't we?"

બ

I shook my head as the three of us walked away. "That really isn't any way to raise a child."

"Quite right," G. agreed. "Spare the rod and spoil the child, that's what I say. How can anyone really expect children to actually do the right thing without hope of reward or fear of punishment?"

"Preposterous!" B. concurred. "Bloody hippies!"

The three of us harrumphed in agreement, and even Monty added a 'whuff' of doggish disapproval as we marched onwards towards our destination.

Chapter 34

On the irrationality of the universe.

We marched on and had not got very far at all when I detected the familiar and dangerous scent of burning tin.

I glanced warily over my shoulder, and saw that B.'s face was screwed up in a veritable storm of concentration. He'd gone bright red and I wasn't sure if I couldn't see steam starting to trickle from his ears.

I thought I'd better release the pressure before he blew and took a sizeable chunk of the countryside, not to mention us, with him.

"A penny for your thoughts old thing?" Expensive at half the price, but never mind.

"It is about," he said heavily, "sandwiches."

"Sandwiches?"

"Well, not really sandwiches."

"You mean sarnies on a more abstract, conceptual level?" G. asked. Trust G. to use words like 'conceptual' in public.

"Conceptual is just the word," B. replied. "The exact bon-bon. It is the concept of sandwiches that I am pondering."

"Go on."

"Right, the question I have been asking myself is this: What makes a sandwich a sandwich, and not a butty?"

G. styles himself as the scientist of our little party, and I turned to him for the answer.

He considered the question for a time. Eventually, he said, "One must first consider carefully the definitions of both. What, for the purposes of this discussion are we to refer to as 'sandwich'. And how are we to differentiate this from butty?"

"It's obvious is it not?" I said. "A sandwich is a filling held between two slices of bread, and consumed in the hands."

"Very well. And a butty?"

"It's... well it's basically the same thing isn't it?"

"But is it?" B. interjected. "I'm not sure."

I frowned. I had meant to maintain a methodical and objective distance from the subject, but I was getting drawn in despite myself. "It's very clear. A butty is served hot, a sandwich is served cold."

"Ah," G. stopped me, raising a finger. "But are toasted sandwiches not served hot as well?"

"Oh. Damn, they are aren't they?" My brow creased. A knotty one indeed! "Well... butties aren't always meat, because of the chip butty... Aha!"

B looked expectantly at me. "You've solved it haven't you? You've solved the great butty-sandwich debate!"

I smiled knowingly. "But of course. The defining feature of a butty is..." I paused to let them hang on my words. I swear that they actually leaned towards me during my perfectly executed dramatic pause.

"The defining feature of a butty is... its grease content."

They paused to consider this, B. nodding as it sunk in.

"Sausage sandwiches," G. said.

"Oh damn!"

"I am beginning to suspect," said B., "that we live in a

beautiful yet bewildering universe, not always bound by rational and rationalistic laws, and that we must accept that there are finite bounds to the limits of human understanding."

G. raised a sceptical eyebrow, but I solemnly agreed. "I think we shall just have to leave the sandwich-butty duality to later generations, whose superior technology and understanding will allow them to determine the nature of sandwichdom, and analyse the exact conditions requisite for buttiality. Alas, I doubt we'll live to see the day when our great-great-great grandchildren solve this greatest of the universe's mysteries."

My stomach gave a sudden and voluble growl, pointing out that if I was going to insist on discussing food, especially the hot, greasy, bread-cased fruits of nature's bounty, then I should convert my words into actions forthwith.

I consulted the map, and discovered that we were practically on top of another village. I awaited it in confident expectation of a sandwich shop.

Chapter 35

On the trappings of long-established denominations.

This thorny philosophical conundrum aside, and my stomach declaring martial law in my abdomen until the current crisis had abated, we trudged forwards.

My map proved itself accurate (for once, as G. unkindly remarked) and within a few minutes we found ourselves passing through another village. Village is a strong word. It might have been a village had the houses all been adjacent, but they were not. They were unsociable houses, who preferred their own company, the dignified old detached houses spurning the society of the chatty little bungalows, and the anxious semi-detacheds clinging nervously together and refusing to talk to anyone else. These were houses that insisted on a field's worth of personal space on either side of them, or they would start to feel stifled.

The gardens were charming, positively war-inducing, and the whole place gave an impression of being well-spaced out, as though every building was lying back and stretching its legs out after a large meal. What it did not give an impression of was any shops whatsoever, never mind a chippy serving dripping bacon baps (which may or may not be butties, pending investigation by future generations). My stomach gave a mutter of bitter frustration and went back to sleep, dormant yet watchful, waiting until the stars were right once more.

As we walked into the vague confines of the settlement, we saw a van trundle past. It was leaving a trail of smelly black smoke, and the engine was grunting and rasping in what could only be its death rattle. I turned to give the driver a stern glare, but my righteous wrath withered as I realised that she was a small, tired-looking old woman, pinched of features, her shoulders slumped and her head bowing.

In the face of this weary, burdened soul, my anger evaporated, and I turned to stare after the van as it laboured painfully away from us. As I did so, I read the sign painted on the side in faded, flaking paint: 'The Shoestring Shelter for the Homeless'.

A little depressed, I turned and hurried after the others, who hadn't bothered to stop. We were only halfway through the dispersed and spacious settlement when we heard a great commotion, a mingled noise of hammering and sawing, and the sound of someone whistling.

Our curiosity whetted, we pressed onwards and found ourselves looking at a strange sight. A house, standing in what might once have been pleasing gardens, but these had now been trampled to muddy mush by the workmen who marched back and forth from a truck, heading around the side of the house to the back. In looking closer, I saw that actually it was two semi-detached houses, although they lacked a fence between their gardens. Looking closer, I could see that both sides had had extensions built on the sides, and additional floors built on the extensions. Some men on scaffolds were now apparently adding an extra floor to the entire building.

I noticed a man leaning against the gatepost of the nearest gate observing the work, and approached him.

"Good afternoon," I said to him politely. He turned and saw me.

"Ah, good afternoon to you, too."

"If you don't mind me asking, what's all this about?" I gestured to the workers.

"Improvements," he replied, "expansions, extensions and additions."

This seemed to me a very thorough answer, but somehow lacking on detail. "What is it you're expanding then?"

He waved vaguely at the houses. "The whole thing."

"I see. You're the foreman then are you?"

He seemed both surprised and amused. "Oh no, I'm the owner. I'm having all of this done."

I peered at the multiple expansions and extensions. "You and your neighbour must have very large families then, or else an awful lot of stuff."

"My neighbour?"

"Whoever lives on the other side."

He stared at me for a second, and then laughed. "Oh, no. That's mine as well. The whole thing belongs to me."

"You must be very rich then," G. remarked, watching the work with a raised eyebrow.

"Oh yes, I am," he replied airily. "Absolutely rolling in it."

"Alright for some," I remarked. "Inherited or self-made man?"

"Neither actually," he said grinning. "It was all given to me."

The three of us stared at each other. "Given?" G. asked

incredulously. "What, all of it?"

"Oh yes. Would you believe that this time three years ago I was penniless? Absolutely destitute and sleeping rough on the streets?"

"Gosh. And some bloke just came along and gave you oodles of cash?"

"That's right. This old bloke. Barmy old geezer. Bit of a local celebrity the way I understand it." My companions and I looked at each other, nodding with sudden understanding.

"Oh, him!" I said. "Yes, we've heard all about him. You couldn't introduce us could you?"

"I'm afraid I very rarely see him," the chap replied apologetically. "But I'll certainly mention you to him next time he's about."

"And this generous old cove just gave you enough money to do all this?" B. asked gesturing at the house.

"Yep. Well, not all at once, no."

"In instalments was it?"

"You could say that, yes. Like I say, I was sleeping rough on the streets, and he comes up to me, and gives me this envelope with three hundred thousand pounds in it, and says 'Up you get my lad. Now go and do something good with that, and I'll be seeing you.'"

"Gosh!" I will happily admit that if I'd realised that that sort of thing happened when you sleep rough, I would have considered it more carefully before deciding to live in a house, let me tell you! "You couldn't tell me what he looks like could you?"

He opened his mouth to reply, but paused. "I... I'm really not sure. I can't remember. I know he was old, but not in an elderly sort of way, if you see what I mean. And he was terribly kind and understanding, but quite, well not fierce as such, but... no, not fierce at all. More sort of... sad really, I think." He fell silent, and stared into space for a few seconds, lost in thought. Then he blinked and shook his head, and gave a little laugh. "Sorry, I really don't remember."

As unsatisfactory as this was, I decided to drop it for the moment. "So you bought a house for yourself then?"

"Yep. Got a mortgage, bought furniture, bought myself some new clothes and things so I could go to job interviews, got myself a job and was doing okay."

The past tense made me frown. "Oh?"

"Well then he comes back to me, and looks around, and nods to himself, sort of pleased like, and says to me, 'Good, I like it. Here's another three hundred thousand. Do something good with it.'"

"Blimey!" B. exclaimed. "Another three hundred thou? Just like that?"

"That's right. Cash in hand and all."

"So what next?"

"Well, I bought the house next door didn't I? I had doors knocked through and doubled the size of the place in one fell swoop. Gave me space for a games room, a film room, a library and guest rooms."

"Do you have many guests to stay?" G. asked with a slight frown.

The fellow shook his head. "Nah. I don't really know that many people, what with having being homeless and all, but it's the kind of thing you ought to have in a big house ain't it?"

"I see," I said, exchanging a look with G. "And then he came back again?"

"Yep. He came back just a month or two ago. Well he looked around, but I don't think he liked it so much as before, but he smiles at me and says, 'Here's a bit more. Now go and do something good with it.' And off he goes again."

"And you've spent it on these extensions?"

"Yep. Lovely job they're doing of it too."

"Yes... So I see."

"And next year, when he brings me the next lot of money, I'm thinking of buying the plot behind and extending the garden." He paused, thinking. "Which sounds better do you think? Summerhouse or gazebo? I was thinking of going posh now I've got money, and I was thinking gazebo sounds ever so bourge-woz."

"Oh, yes. I suppose it does rather," I replied weakly.

"Have you ever," G. asked suddenly, "heard of an establishment called 'The Shoestring Shelter for the Homeless'?"

The chap frowned. "Oh, yeah. Yeah, I had to kip there a few times me'self. Terrible place that! All musty and run down, and the bed sheets worn so thin you can nearly see through'em. Nah, wouldn't catch me touching a place like that now. Not now I'm rich!"

"You don't suppose," G. went on, "that when the old gentleman told you to do something good with the money, that he didn't mean buy two houses and add extensions?"

The fellow's frown deepened. "Like what? Seems pretty good to me?"

I'd caught onto G.'s train of thought by now, and weighed in. "How many rooms did you say this house has?"

"Oh, well, including the games room, the DVD cinema, the dining room, the library, the den, the two bathrooms, two kitchens, living room, master bedroom and the three spare bedrooms, um..." he counted on his fingers. "Fourteen."

"And there's just you living there?"

"That's right."

"And that strikes you as being right does it? That's what you think the generous old millionaire wanted when he gave you all that money and told you to 'do good'?"

"Well I did, didn't I? This house is great! I've got everything I ever wanted." He started to become angry. "And I deserve it! I was homeless! I was cold, and starving and alone! I deserve to have a house, and furniture, and nice clothes and good food! I deserve it!"

"Well yes, quite possibly, but don't you think that once you had a house and decent clothes, you should have started using it to help others?"

"Why the hell should I? No one's ever helped me!"

"Except the old gentleman," G. pointed out firmly.

The man opened his mouth to reply, and then shut it with a snap. "Yeah, but..." He trailed off, glared at us, turned on his heel and marched straight through the front door, which he shut behind him with a loud bang.

The three of us looked at each other, shrugged and turned back to our road, the sounds of hammers and saws gradually fading behind us.

Chapter 36

On the dual nature of Christ.

Only a very short time later, as we marched doggedly along the road, we passed over a bridge across a little stream. Next to the stream sat a young man. He was wearing a baggy, old-looking coat, and faded jeans, and had long hair done up in dreadlocks. He held an unpeeled orange in his hand, and was staring at it with an expression of supreme concentration, tinged with puzzlement.

I paused to watch him, and as I did so, he sighed, shook his head, leant down and dipped his other hand in the stream. He stared at this instead, and then, after a few seconds, during which he wiggled his fingers about underwater, he took it out again and wiped it on his trousers. I decided that he must be a philosopher, and I voiced this speculation to my comrades.

G. nodded. "Possibly. It's so hard to tell nowadays. Time was that philosophers were all bearded older gentlemen in togas, or possibly bath towels, so they were easy to spot."

B frowned. "I've never been certain of the difference between a toga and a bath towel. Is there one?"

"Oh yes," G. said authoritatively. "A toga is worn across the shoulder. A both towel is worn around the waist."

"But women tend to wear them up around their chests

without going over the shoulder," I pointed out.

"That is because women confuse things. They put them on their heads like turbans as well. It's why they're not allowed to be philosophers."

"My aunt used to have a fellow who looked a lot like that chap there lodging with her," B. announced, "and she said he was a philosopher. At least, he said a lot of strange things, and there was this strange smell coming from his room. My mother used to refer to him as 'the herbaceous boarder', and didn't seem to approve at all. He certainly didn't smell like he ever used a bath towel!"

I watched as the suspected philosopher stared in bewilderment at the orange. Eventually, my elephantine 'satiable curtiosity got the better of me, and leaning against the rail, I looked down at him.

"Pardon me."

The young man looked up at me, blinking in surprise as he swam up out of the ocean of deep thought he had been immersing himself in, diving for pearls of wisdom. "Hmmm? Oh, hello." I was a little surprised to find him well-spoken.

"If you don't mind me asking, what's so fascinating about the orange?"

"I don't understand it." He sighed, and glared ferociously at the offending fruit. "It doesn't make any sense at all!"

"Oh, really? They've always seemed fairly straight forward to me."

The chap shook his head emphatically, sending his dreadlocks whipping back and forth. "Not at all! How can this be?" He held up the guilty fruit accusingly. I peered at it, but it appeared to be a perfectly standard orange.

"What's causing the brain-ache then?"

"You're aware that things have a nature I suppose?"

"I think so, yes. Some more so than others in fact," I added, glancing at Monty. "Some things are positively brimming over with nature."

"Well it seems like some things are more than one thing at once. And that doesn't make sense!"

"Right..." I looked at my companions, who shrugged. They didn't seem to care about the Orange Question at all.

"I mean," the young fellow continued, "this orange is entirely orange, right?"

"It's undeniable," I agreed, "that that orange is orange in colour. Whether the fruit is named for the hue or vice versa though, I couldn't tell you."

"Okay, but the orange is also round."

"It is, yes. Not actually spherical, but definitely rounded."

"But how!?"

I frowned. "How what?"

"How can it be both? Its nature must be one of roundness, or one of orangeness!"

"Surely, it's both.

"Nonsense!" He paused, looking at me warily. "You're not about to go all quantum are you? I can't stand it when people go all quantum!"

"I don't think so. Possibly it's something that just happens, sort of comes over you if you see what I mean."

"Right. Very well then. Carry on."

"Thank you. Now where was I? Ah, yes. Of course oranges are round as well as orange. Look at that one there, just to give an example." He peered at it suspiciously, and even gave it a shake, to see what would happen. Nothing, as it turned out.

"Now, to my mind, shape and colour are completely different, and can't be compared. Apples and oranges as it were. Not, actually that you can't compare apples and oranges, come to think of it. I mean, one can point out that the orange is not an apple," I continued, "or an aardvark, or a Porsche convertible. Again, if it is one, it cannot be any of the others. That is because you are discussing different categories of physical object, but that means that they are all physical objects." The philosopher nodded.

"And one can have an orange, and say that it is three inches across, which means that it can't be four inches across, or two and a half. It must be one or the other. You are discussing magnitudes of the same dimension."

Again, he nodded.

"But," I went on, "shape and colour are totally different dimensions. They cannot be compared. I am not taller than I am pink, nor am I paler than I am short. In this case, I will humbly submit that this fruit that you hold is both wholly round, and wholly orange, of single and indivisible nature, and if all you're going to do is sit and stare at it, I'll take it off your hands and put it to good use."

༺

As we walked away, me peeling my orange, G. gave me a look. After a few seconds, he asked, "J. why is it that you've given so much thought to oranges?"

"Oh, well you know. Back at uni, I worked in the fruit and veg aisle of the local supermarket. You'd be amazed at what your brain latches onto to avoid starvation. Would you like to hear my Grand Theory of Courgettes?"

"No. No, I don't think so."

"Oh. Right ho."

We continued on our way.

214

Chapter 37

That you can only disregard certain of and so many elements of Christianity before what you have left isn't worth having.

Hiding the hurt inflicted by this show of wilful ignorance regarding the Courgette Conundrum, we carried on for a bit, until, passing out of the next village, I saw worrying signs of impending doom.

One reads occasionally of the preternaturally acute senses, or perhaps the supernaturally prescient instincts, of the lower orders of the phyla Mammalia and um... Bird...alia. Ornitho-thingy. Birds. Fish as well possibly, although I wouldn't really know. Anyway, one hears about how the lower vertebrates can predict earthquakes and tidal waves and whatnot and get out sharpish before the disaster strikes, while the higher mind of Man, distracted as it is by algebra, philosophy and the Inland Revenue, fails to notice the warning signs and gets volcanoed or washed away just as it finishes its tax return.

Well, I'd paid my taxes for the year, so I was able to apprehend the danger in a second-hand sort of way, by keen observation of the birds and animals. Normally, wisely fearing the stern hand of man, creatures will shy away, but those beasts that have been subjugated by the yoke, the bridle and the collar have grown used to our bipedal idiosyncrasies, and instead of sensibly fleeing, will instead approach us in expectation of fresh hay or a pat on the nose.

However, the cows and sheep of nearby fields did not come near. A pair of horses did not approach in hope of sugar lumps or a mint. Instead, every item of livestock in the vicinity was pressed up against fences and hedges at the furthest extremity of each field as we passed. Birds in the trees took wing and whizzed away as fast as their little wings could carry them. Had a hungry panther of the type known to swarm in the quieter parts of England come upon us then, I have no doubt that it would have turned tail and fled. I turned and found even Monty, who normally has an air most generously described as 'furtive', cowering as far from us as the length of his extendable lead would allow.

To be quite frank, it struck me as rather ominous. I was about to comment on my observations when the event struck, and we were slap bang on ground zero.

With a roar that set beasts and birds shrieking, and car alarms for miles around lifting their voices in warning chorus, B.'s stomach rumbled.

Now don't think I exaggerate. 'Surely', you will say, 'B.'s stomach has rumbled before, and it didn't strike us at the time as cataclysmic.' And you would be right to say so, dear reader. Indeed, in these pages B.'s alimentary utterings have been likened to whale song and distant thunder. Well, all I can say is that this was on a different level of magnitude to those gentle digestive murmurings. It shook and staggered us, made our ears pop and set our teeth a-rattling. No permanent structural damage appeared to have been caused to our surroundings, but a seven-point earthquake and accompanying tsunami hit the western coastline of North America about an hour later. B. denies all responsibility, but I say that if a butterfly can cause a hurricane on the other side of the world with the draught from its wings, then B. can certainly cause an earthquake with his abdominal oscillations.

When the dust had settled, and G. and I had picked ourselves up again, B. turned to us, and without the slightest trace of irony said, "I say chaps, I'm starting to get a bit peckish."

G. and I looked at each other. We looked back at B. and decided that for the sake of global safety and the continued survival of western civilisation it was our duty to stop for a bite to eat.

Happily, no aftershocks occurred for the thirty minutes or so that it took for us to reach the next bastion of rural civilisation. But what minutes they were! At every moment I was expecting the seas to boil and rise up, the mountains to crumble and the sky to fall about my ears! A pigeon took off very suddenly from a tree next to the road, and I can only attribute the fact that I did not suffer a coronary arrest to clean living, good diet and exercise. Whose clean living, good diet and exercise I'm sure I don't know, but I am indebted to them nonetheless.

Suffice to say that I was a broken, nervous wreckage of my former self by the time we arrived at the pleasant little café in the next village, and in dire need of a little something myself. G. looked little better and was clutching Monty protectively to his chest lest the End Times come suddenly.

We stepped into the charming eatery and were instantly assailed by a wave of delicious aromas that set our mouths watering and our stomachs rumbling. I winced, but no seismic forces were unleashed, and with the moment of crisis past, we went to place our orders. There was a fellow in front of us, and as we stood salivating over the standard arsenal of buns, cakes, pastries, baked potatoes, and toasted sandwiches, I couldn't help but overhear him.

"I'll have some of the chicken stew please."

No sooner had I heard these fateful words than I knew that if I needed anything to eat at all, it was chicken stew. I felt that I would sicken, wither away and die if I didn't have chicken stew within minutes. Such are the thoughts wrought on the brain by a copious and demanding stomach.

"Ahhhh... Chicken stew," I murmured raptly. I heard an in-drawn breath behind me. "Chicken stew..." G. whispered, his voiced heavy with longing. "Mmm... chicken stew," came the fainter murmur, almost drowned out by an anticipatory gurgle from his stomach as B. contemplated the possibility of hot stew.

And so it came to pass that, five minutes later, the three of us were seated at a small table, bowls of steaming stew and crusty buttered rolls before us. Monty was tied up outside and seemed to be contentedly dozing in the sun, the food smelled good, and we prepared to get stuck in.

Now I do not consider myself to be an overly fussy eater. There are still a few things I severely dislike, but this list has contracted considerably since I was a young and finicky little thing who, with his back to the wall and believing in the justice of his cause, would hide his peas in a nearby pot plant when no one was looking so as to avoid eating them. (That pot plant sickened and died soon afterwards, I might add. Vindication!) Nowadays, I am more accepting, and will eat a great many things that I abhorred and abominated as a youngster. However, there are still lines that one must never cross, even as one gets older, jaded, and more tolerant of the evils of this fallen world of ours, and such a line has been drawn before onions.

I do not like onions. I understand that many do, and good luck to them, but I do not try and force them to stop eating onions, and I will thank them not to try and force the foetid things down my throat. I have, it is true, immunised myself to some extent by taking very small amounts frequently, so that now I suspect that I could survive quite a significant dose, although I have no wish to put this to the test.

This being so, I started carefully fishing out the largest chunks of the foul and slimy stuff from my stew. Just the big chunks mind you. I am willing to concede that a great many dishes are improved by the addition of onion, *so long as you cannot taste the onion itself.* Added to what I said above about immunising myself to their ill-effects, I am happy to leave the smaller pieces in situ. I placed the large pieces of onion on the side plate, being careful not to cross-contaminate my bread roll.

Having done this, I set about doing the same thing to the mushroom. I don't mind mushroom too much, and certainly not nearly as much as onion. It's the texture more than anything else that I dislike, and again I am quite happy to leave the smaller pieces where they are, just fishing out the largest and most unavoidable chunks. These I passed over to G., who is a great eater of mushrooms, and he accepted them gratefully.

G. doesn't like parsnip, and these he had fished out and handed over to B. B. is a bottomless pit, a gastronomic black hole that sucks in food of all kinds, countries and flavours. He shows no mercy, takes no prisoners and leaves none alive to bear news of disaster to the relatives of the lost.

Quite happy with what we had before us, we set to with gusto and. for a while, the only sound to be heard from our table was the contented slurping and munching of three grown men refuelling body, mind and soul.

I was just scooping up the last little bits of vegetable and little scraps of chicken from the bottom of the bowl when I happened to glance up and saw the man who had been in front of us in the queue. He was bent over his bowl, apparently examining the contents carefully. On the side plate, next to the as-yet untouched bread roll was a small mound of food. Peering across, I could make out onion, mushroom, parsnip, potato, and as I watched, he fished out some pearl barley and deposited it neatly on top of the pile.

He carefully dipped his spoon in again and extracted a little more of the barley. As he did so, he looked up and saw me staring at me. His eyes flickered down to the pile of vegetables on the side plate, and he gave me a weak smile.

"I don't really like vegetables," he explained with a slight, self-deprecating laugh. "I always have to pick them out."

"Ah," I said nodding. "I'm not a big fan of onion myself. Or mushrooms."

The man pulled a face. "Ugh! Onions! No, foul stuff! It should be banned as a harmful substance if you ask me! I do like chicken stew though, which is why I'm willing to go through this whole malarkey to get it."

This was an opinion that I could agree with, but it still seemed rather strange behaviour. "But do you not think that it's rather less than chicken stew if you take out most of the ingredients?"

"Not really. I understand that some people like to have all of the extra little bits and pieces, but I find that they distract from the central flavour of the dish."

"That seems fair," I pondered this for a few seconds. "But don't you feel you're not really getting your money's worth?"

"I suppose not, but I do love chicken stew, and the stew from this place really is the best I've ever had. I come here quite often just for the chicken stew."

I nodded. It really was excellent stuff, and I turned back to scraping up the very last morsels from the bottom of my bowl.

I had done so and was sitting back and holding my stomach in warm and pleasant contentment when I looked back across at our neighbour. I blinked and looked again. He had still not started eating, and was now picking out pieces of chicken and depositing these on the plate beside the discarded vegetables. He once more glanced up, slightly guiltily I thought, and saw me looking again.

"I don't really care for chicken," he admitted, somewhat sheepishly.

"You don't really care for chicken?" I repeated.

"Not really, no."

"But you like chicken stew?"

"Oh yes! Love the stuff!"

"And you don't like onion, mushroom, parsnip or pearl barley?"

"Not really, no, but I don't consider them essential to the stew."

"Is chicken not essential to chicken stew?"

"I don't really think so, no. More essential than the vegetables perhaps, but still not absolutely necessary."

A short while later, while we waited for the puddings to arrive, I glanced back over at him as he picked the last little scrap of meat out and deposit it neatly on the now considerable pile. In his bowl, I could see that he had a thin, clear liquid which had gone quite cold and congealed. He took a spoonful and put it in his mouth, smacking his lips with every appearance of satisfaction.

Once more, he caught me staring. "I do love chicken stew!" he said happily. I shook my head in bafflement, and looked away.

Chapter 38

Why some level of organised religion is still important.

I looked away from this curious creature with his colourless, flavourless and un-nutritious fluid, glancing around the café in an attempt to spot some sanity somewhere. Even a little bit would have done.

In one corner a man and two women were sitting at a table, food before them. One of the women had opted for the stew, the other had gone for a panini of some kind, while the man had what looked like a cheese and ham toastie.

I sighed contentedly. They looked like perfectly sane people, and two, the man and one of the women at least were stylish in the extreme, wearing sunglasses despite being indoors.

But as I watched, my heart sank slightly. I could see that something odd was at work here. The lady without sunglasses leaned forwards and spoke to the other two, glancing down at their plates from time to time. I strained my ears to catch what she was saying. Rude I know, but that's what happens when you have that elephantine 'satiable curtiosity that I mentioned before. G. calls it nosiness. I call it having an observant and enquiring mind, and a keen interest in the world in which I live.

"...lovely golden brown," she was saying to the man. She used her knife and fork to carefully prise open his toastie. "The cheese is a deep, rich yellow, and the ham is lovely and pink. It's steaming and the cheese is good and melted all the way through." She turned to the other woman. "Your panini is slightly toasted, with little dark lines across the top from the grill. The salad with it is very nice. The red onions are a beautiful deep burgundy, the grated carrot is almost glowing, and the lettuce is a very pale green, almost white, with little droplets of moisture on it."

Comprehension suddenly dawned. The two stylish people were not stylish at all, or if they were, it wasn't the reason they were wearing sunglasses indoors. They were blind. I wondered, for B.'s sake, if I should ask them whether they'd ever been allowed to go and stroke an elephant. I decided against it. They might think that I was some sort of weirdo. They might not be wrong of course, but that's not really the point.

I was about to turn away, when the blind man leaned forwards over the sighted woman's stew and inhaled deeply through his nose. "Mmmmm," he sighed. It smells beautiful. The chicken is just right, with a little hint of saltiness, and the herbs are just right, not too strong. The vegetables smell wonderful, quite sweet." He turned to the other woman's panini, leaned over that and breathed in. "Yes, cranberry and brie. The cranberries have just the right sharpness and sweetness, the brie is wonderfully ripe, perhaps a touch too strong, but absolutely wonderful nonetheless. The salad smells fresh and sweet, I can smell the moisture on the lettuce."

I frowned as the first woman, the sighted one, leaned

across the table and used her knife and fork to cut away a piece of the man's toastie, without so much as a by-your-leave. A vile thing I call it, stealing food from in front of a blind chap. I was about to get up and give her a piece of my mind, but what happened next made me pause.

The sighted woman put the fork into the hand of the blind woman who instantly put it in her mouth and crunched it, rolling it around in her mouth and chewing slowly. "Oh, yes, it's lovely. The toast is good, it tastes well-done, almost burnt around the crust, but just right in the middle, the cheese is mature and quite sharp, and the ham is slightly salty and smoky."

The sighted woman then took a spoonful of her stew, and passed it to the blind woman, who blew on it to cool it, then put it in her mouth, tasting it carefully again before swallowing. "Oh, yes," she said, "yes, that is beautiful. The chicken is wonderful, really tender and juicy, and the vegetables are perfect. Not too soft and with all their sweetness and flavour intact. The dumplings are floury and firm. Beautiful."

They all smiled, and sat quietly for a few moments before suddenly all tucking in with a gusto that warmed my heart to see. While I had been observing these goings on, our puddings had arrived and been dutifully assaulted with élan and panache; swiftly we ate and well, and soon those puddings were no more, and the world was safe once again from the tectonic disturbances of B.'s digestive tract. For an hour or so at any rate.

As we prepared to continue on our pilgrimage, I couldn't resist going over and talking to the strange trio. "Pardon me," I said, "but I couldn't help overhearing you. Do you mind me asking what it's all about?"

They smiled politely at me. "Not at all," the blind woman said. "You see Matthew and I are both blind. Deborah here is our friend, and brings us out every so often to go and eat somewhere. We can't see the food, so Deborah describes it to us, so that we can imagine what it is we're eating."

"That's jolly decent of you, Deborah, but what was the business with Matthew here smelling your food?"

Deborah nodded. "Ah, well you see Mary and I have no sense of smell. Matthew describes the smells for us, so that we can imagine what they are like."

"Right..." I said slowly, beginning to understand, "And you and Matthew have no sense of taste?"

"That's right. So Mary tries a little bit of our food and describes the tastes. Matthew and I can both feel the texture of the food, and with Mary's help we can imagine the taste at the same time."

"So of the three of you, only one of you can see, only one of you can smell and only one of you can taste?"

"Correct. But by coming together like this and sharing our different perspectives of a common experience, we all get a wider and more complete image of what it is that's before us."

"That's rather wonderful," I replied. "Thank you very much for explaining it to me. Enjoy your meals."

B. and G. had already left and were waiting for me outside. "You know," I said thoughtfully, "people can surprise you by what they're capable of when they put their heads together."

"True," G. said, "but sometimes they need to be banged together first to get them into position."

"Very often I think. Shall we continue?"

"We shall." And off we went.

Chapter 39

Our destination? Thoughts on continual grace.

Finally, after days of weary toil, the spires and roofs of Canterbury could finally be seen looming over the horizon, and it was with a sense of relief and satisfaction that we beheld the object of our pilgrimage-cum-walking holiday.

It is neither my intention nor my desire to write a travel guide or tourist-board pamphlet. If you do want information about various bishops and a-Beckets and Marlowes and museums and about the cathedral itself, then I can only ask that you look elsewhere, inquisitive reader, for you shall find none here.

I have to confess that I was a little disappointed by what I found upon reaching Canterbury. Although intellectually aware that it was a perfectly modern town, I had still, somewhere in the back of my mind, expected it to be more... well, Chaucerian. More black and white timber buildings and whatnot. Obviously there are a few of these around, but nonetheless the industrial estates and office blocks and houses of a modern British town were a considerable, if not really unexpected, let-down.

Trying to deal with my grief and disappointment in as

manly and stoical a way as I could manage, I stiffened my lip and lengthened my stride. My companions started to lag behind me, and were forced to quicken their pace to catch up.

"I say J.," B. gasped, "what's the hurry? We're nearly there! Slow down a bit would you, there's a stout fellow."

I bit my tongue to restrain the obvious response, and made a conscious effort to slow down. My colleagues laboured up to me, B. puffing like bellows. I paused awhile as my two comrades-in-adventure caught their breath. I am not, I freely confess, much of a health-and-fitness sort of a chap, but I have been blessed with a highly efficient metabolism and what can be best described as 'rude good health' in the best sense of the term.

I turned to carry onwards into the town and very nearly ran slap bang into a young woman, only narrowly avoiding knocking her down by a most undignified twist of my body and a staggering hop to the side.

"Oh, I am most terribly sorry!" I started to say, but stopped, staring at the girl with undisguised horror. She was pretty enough in a slender sort of way, but this fact was very much detracted from by the two black eyes and considerable swelling around her face.

"My dear girl!" I exclaimed. "What on earth has happened to you?" G. and B. were also gazing with mingled horror and pity at this poor injured creature.

She half-raised a hand to her face, but stopped. One might have expected a person in such a situation to be embarrassed perhaps, or at least rather shy, but she seemed to make no bones about hiding her injuries.

"My husband," she said simply. "He hit me."

Now then, it has in the past been said to me that chivalry is really terribly old-fashioned, and what was once referred to as 'gentlemanly behaviour' is now considered rather sexist and ignorant. Well then I confess myself an ignorant and sexist chauvinist dinosaur of the worst possible stripe, because her words caused a cold and terrible fury to boil up inside me. I was brought up in an old-fashioned sort of a household, and all the codes of chivalry and gentlemanly conduct can for me be summarised in three commandments. Tell the truth; be decent to others; and under no circumstances whatsoever are you ever to hit girls.

"He... hit you?" I said rather quietly. G. and B. exchanged worried glances. They knew about my rather broad quixotic streak, and were wary of it.

The woman nodded. "Yes, he did. It's okay though."

"Okay?"

She nodded again and smiled. "Yes, it's okay. You don't need to worry about me."

"My dear woman," I cried, "this thug has brutalised you! Do you have anywhere to go? Relatives or friends?"

"Oh yes, plenty of both, thank you. But look, you really mustn't worry about me. I know it sounds strange but I really do have the situation under control. I'm going home now."

"I should hope so! Change the locks and don't ever let him darken your doorstep again!"

"Oh, no. He'll calm down, and realise what it is he's done, and then he'll come and apologise, and ask me to take him back."

"Well possibly, but surely now you know what sort of man he is, that's hardly likely." Her expression made me hesitate. "Is it?"

She smiled. "This isn't the first time this has happened, and I daresay that it won't be the last. I've taken him back before, and I'll keep taking him back."

I shook my head. One hears, occasionally, of these poor confused women who love a man even though he continually hurts them, how sometimes they become convinced that they even deserve that hurt, and how they are unwilling to see what a vile brute it is that they have attached themselves to until one day he goes too far and she is killed. I wanted to reach out and embrace this woman, to protect her, but once more I saw that she was smiling.

"I know what you're thinking," she said calmly, "You think that I'm deluded or emotionally confused or something. It really isn't like that at all."

"I see," I said, perhaps more caustically than I had intended. "He beats you because he really does love you?"

"No. He beats me because he is ignorant and weak and small and scared."

I snorted. "And this fine example of manhood is why you're going back to endure more violence?"

She gave me an odd look. "It's why I'm going back, yes. Think about it."

I snorted again.

"He's ignorant, and weak, and small and scared. Can you think of any person who needs help, who needs love, more than someone like that?"

"I can think of a great many people who deserve love a great deal more than that!"

"Deserve? Yes, I suppose he doesn't deserve it. But if everybody in the world only received what they deserved, then don't you think that we'd all be in a lot of trouble? Do you really deserve what you have?"

I was about to retort with some cutting riposte, but paused. I glanced at B. and G. for support, but they shrugged. They were leaving this one wholly to me. Cowards.

230

"I see where you're going with this," I conceded, "but…"

"It is exactly people like him who need help, who need love, and it is precisely because he does not deserve it that I am prepared to put up with this, no matter how much it hurts, no matter how often he pushes me away and hits me. I will love him, even if he doesn't want it, even if he doesn't deserve it, even if he doesn't know it, because in the end he needs it. He needs my help, and if I keep offering, then one day he will open his eyes, and accept it, and become a new person because of it."

And then I realised what she was talking about. I had, I must admit, been thinking of her as confused, as pitiable, indeed as incredibly weak. It had seemed to me that she must have been rather wet, rather a push-over to keep accepting this vile wretch back, despite his horrendous transgressions, but now I began to understand that it wasn't weakness that I was seeing. It was a patience, a perseverance, dare I say it, a grace that only looked like weakness. On closer inspection, it turned out to be the most powerful and wonderful strength.

Humbled, I nodded and stepped aside to let her continue on her way, much to my friends' surprise.

"I think," I said after a few minute's silence, "that we are getting very close now. I think we're nearly there." And with that, I turned and continued walking towards through the town, albeit at a slightly more sedate pace to allow for B. and G., and even little Monty.

Chapter 40

We arrive. Financial difficulties and an unexpected obstacle.

As we pushed on through Canterbury, my heart continued to sink. It was just as noisy and smelly and thoroughly modern as any other town I'd ever been to. True there was a nice building here and there, and overall it was far nicer than a lot of places I've been to, but nonetheless, my disappointment continued unabated. My own fault, I know, for having such unrealistic expectations about our destination.

There was traffic, and there were jostling, hurrying people, and all the usual bland and boring shops you'd expect to see in any town in the country, and there were the same homeless people sitting by the pavement, caps in front of them, or standing in the way trying to sell the Big Issue.

An old fellow in a filthy coat and fingerless gloves caught my eye. "Any spare change mate?" he muttered hopelessly. I shook my head and mumbled an apology, hurrying onwards with my head down. I paused and considered my action. Surely, given the nature of the journey we had undertaken, I should do something to help the chap?

"Don't you do it J.," G. said severely, noticing me hesitate.

"But surely we should…"

"We should do nothing of the sort. He'd only spend it on booze."

"Well I could buy him a sandwich or something then couldn't I?"

"He might not like it," B. pointed out. "He might have allergies or something."

"You know what they say," G. continued sternly, "You're much better off donating to a homeless charity. At least that way you know that the money is being spent on something worthwhile."

"I suppose so…" I said reluctantly, allowing myself to be ushered off. As we walked, I repeated G. and B.'s arguments in my head until they seemed like sense (a first, I'm sure!) and the guilt at not doing anything for the poor chap had faded to a vague niggling at the back of my mind.

We could see the mighty tower of the cathedral looming above us. As we got closer and closer, I began to feel excited, and even a little bit nervous. We were coming to the end of our journey, and I tried to decide if I felt any better, morally and spiritually that is, than when I'd began so many days before. I wasn't honestly sure that I did. In fact, the opposite seemed to be true. I was now more aware of how far I had to go than when I'd started. Despite having walked for so many days, I now rather felt like I was only just becoming aware of how much further I had to go, just when I thought I was almost there.

I have already said that it is not my intention to write this as a travel guide, or at least not the normal sort in any case, and so I shall not burden you, or do a grave injustice to the edifice itself, by attempting a description of the cathedral. We reached the mighty doors, and craned our necks backwards to look up at the building rearing above us.

I took a deep breath, and turned to my companions. "Right," I said, "shall we?"

"Is there anything we're supposed to do?" G. asked, glancing at the cathedral doors apprehensively. "Do we have to let them know that we're pilgrims or anything?"

"Perhaps they'll have special refreshments for pilgrims..." B. said wistfully.

G. snorted. "Oh yes, maybe big slabs of communion bread, served by vestal virgins and washed down with holy water with ambrosia for pudding!"

B. perked up at this. "Ambrosia rice pudding?"

"No! I..." G. sighed. "Never mind B. Shall we go in?"

I nodded, and with a certain amount of trepidation, the three of us passed though into the cathedral. Inside it was cool and spacious, echoing and quiet. There were quite a few people wandering about, peering at stained-glass windows and carvings and whatnot.

"Huh," I said with a slight sneer. "Tourists!"

G. shook his head. "Sad really aren't they? They have no purity of purpose."

"You can see it can't you?" B. agreed. "No purity of purpose at all. It's quite obvious when you look at them."

"Something about the way they carry themselves," I concurred. "The way they hold themselves, as though their purposes are utterly contaminated." The three of us unconsciously tried to stand a little straighter and hold our heads a little higher, as befitting the purity of our purpose. Even Monty contrived to look a little less ratty.

"Mind you," B. said after a moment, "impurity of purpose isn't always a bad thing. Do you remember Mabel Figworthy, from uni J.? The night down the union when you drank that blue stuff? Her purposes were downright..."

"Yes, thank you, B.! We are in a church you know. I think we..." I trailed off as my eye alighted on something rather puzzling. "I say you chaps... what's that?"

They looked at where I was pointing, and both paused, frowning.

"Well..." G. began uncertainly, "it looks a bit like a turnstile."

"That's what I thought too," B. agreed, and we all frowned at it. It certainly appeared to be a turnstile, next to a glass-fronted booth, in which an attendant sat. Examining it more closely, I realised that it represented the only opening through a barrier preventing us from getting much further inside.

"I'm sure it's just a mistake," I said with a confidence I admit to not possessing in reality. "I'll go and talk to the lady."

I walked up to the booth and smiled at her. "Um, excuse me, my friends and I need to get through." I gestured at the turnstile and smiled apologetically.

She smiled back. "Of course sir. Are you a pre-booked group?"

"Um, no, not really. That is, we knew we were coming. We didn't realise you had to book a pew or anything."

"You don't have to sir, but it is a little cheaper."

"Cheaper?"

"Yes sir. It's seven pounds fifty a head for a pre-booked group. I'm afraid that'll be nine pounds for each of you please."

I hesitated and scratched my head, slightly confused. "I don't have to pay nine pounds to get into the church at home..." I said.

"No sir, probably not."

"Yes, right. Erm, this _is_ a church isn't it?"

"Oh yes sir, but our upkeep costs are extremely high, so we charge admission."

"Right... right. One moment." I returned to my friends.

"They want to charge us nine pounds each to get in," I told them.

"Oh," G. seemed quite taken aback. B. was similarly stumped.

"Perhaps it would help if they knew we were pilgrims?" he suggested. "Tell them about our purity of purpose."

"Good idea!" G. agreed. "The charge is probably just for tourists and people come to gawk at tombs and such. I imagine that pilgrims are allowed straight through."

I nodded and returned to the booth. "Hello again." The lady smiled at me once more. "Yes, well, you see we _are_ pilgrims you know. We've walked all the way here, and it seems a bit off to be charging us to get in, now that we're here."

"I'm sorry sir," she said in a slightly firmer tone of voice, "but everyone has to pay, unless they're attending a service."

"Ah, I see. Any services on at the moment?"

"No sir."

"Right... It seems a bit off, doesn't it, charging people to get into a church? Money lenders in the temple and so forth?"

She was now looking at me with unmistakable disapproval, and it occurred to me that I might not be the first person to point this out. Muttering imprecations quite unsuitable for an ecclesiastical setting, I returned to my friends once more.

"Nothing doing. Apparently pilgrims have to pay as well."

"Ah. I suppose we'll have to then," G. said reluctantly.

"Now that we're here and all."

"I suppose so, yes."

Somewhat morosely, we reached into our pockets for our wallets. I opened mine and blinked. The place in my wallet where my money usually sat, beaming up at me with a friendly and welcoming expression, was empty. Not so much as a solitary fiver to greet my eye. I frowned. Prior to setting forth on our expedition, I had taken a considerable amount of cash out of the bank for purposes of subsistence, and possibly souvenirs, if I found anything suitable. Where could it have all gone?

I glanced up to see G. frowning in consternation at the inside of his own wallet, which I could see presented a bleak and deserted landscape equal to mine. He looked up at me and saw my expression. He glanced at my wallet and raised an eyebrow.

"But where can it have all gone?" I asked plaintively.

He thought for a moment. "Well there was that pub. We had a couple of drinks there. And a meal. Then that other pub. A meal there too. With drinks. Another pub. Food and refreshments. A tavern. Dinner and a pint. The fast-food place. An inn. Lunch and a tankard or so there I think. That supermarket. The village shop. A pub or two more. The campsite. Then that pub of course..."

"Ah, yes. I can see how it trickled away."

"Yes... Perhaps we should have spent less time in pubs?"

"Perhaps so." I turned to B. "I say, B. old thing, any chance you could stand G. and I a tenner each?" I paused as he looked at me wide-eyed, patting his pockets frantically. He wriggled out of his backpack and started rifling through that as well.

"What on earth's the matter?"

"It's gone!"

"What's gone?"

"My wallet! I swear I had it this morning, but now it's gone!"

"That's not at all good," I admitted. "You're sure?"

"Yes, blast it! It's completely vanished!"

I chuckled. "Poor old B." I said to G. "I've always said he was careless, and that he should take more care of his things."

"Yes well you shouldn't be laughing, J." B snapped. "I had the train tickets in there!"

My chuckles died on my lips. Naturally we had been planning on walking to Canterbury. It wouldn't really have been a pilgrimage otherwise, but we had determined at the start that we would be returning via more agreeable methods. That and we only had so much time off work, and a walk back would have taken us outside our probation.

"Have you checked all of your pockets?" I asked, my voice a little shaky.

"Yes, confound it! It's gone, and they're gone, and we're stuck!"

"Well surely we don't have to go further into the cathedral?" G. asked. "I mean, we've reached it, and we're inside. We've completed the pilgrimage haven't we?"

"I don't know," I replied, "I rather assumed that we'd have to do some praying at the altar or something. Mark the occasion."

"I don't know about that! Praying in public? I'd feel like a complete fool, doing that where people could see me!"

"But surely people won't mind if you do it in a cathedral, where the children can't see it."

"No, I think we've completed our pilgrimage. We ought to go, since we aren't rich enough to enter."

I was about to respond when an attendant-looking gentleman approached us. "I beg your pardon sirs, but I'm afraid you must take your dog outside. No animals allowed inside the cathedral."

G. was about to respond, and poorly if I am any judge of my companion, but I interrupted him. "I am terribly sorry," I said to the fellow, "I really didn't think it would be a problem."

"You thought that we'd allow dogs to wander around inside the cathedral?"

"Oh no, of course not. I thought that he'd burst into flames the moment he set a paw on holy ground. I thought we'd just be left with a pile of ashes and an empty collar and lead to deal with."

"Montgomery and I are leaving!" G. snapped at me. He scooped the insufferable hound up and marched out of the doors. I gave the attendant a smile and followed after him, accompanied by B.

"Just imagine not allowing dogs!" G. was muttering. "Why I wouldn't want to be a member of any religion that didn't allow Monty as a member!"

"That restricts you to Satanism then, or possibly one of the Ancient Egyptian cults if I recall correctly. Actually, that might have been a jackal..."

"Well we're here now, in Canterbury, with no money, unable to actually get into the cathedral that we've walked all the way here just to get into, and we have no way of getting home again."

"I am willing to admit that everything hasn't quite gone according to plan..."

B. ambled up to us. "It has been a disaster. I suppose we'll have to phone someone at home and see if they can come and pick us up. It shouldn't take too long to get here by car, and I'm sure we can pay for petrol once we're home."

"Certainly not!" I cried, aghast. "Admit to such a horrendous mistake? Death first!"

G. nodded. To have to admit such an appalling series of oversights, especially to female acquaintances already sceptical about the existence of our collective common sense, would have been nothing short of disastrous. We would have dishonoured our entire gender, quislings in the battle of the sexes. I could hear their 'I told you so's' ringing in my ears even now.

"Out of the question," G. said firmly. "We shall find some way of surviving here, and of escaping, all by ourselves."

"Just like Robinson Crusoe, when he was stranded in hostile terrain!" I agreed. I wondered if we could build some sort of house out of palm branches. Looking around what I could see of Canterbury town centre though, not a single palm tree was to be found.

"Well, perhaps we could amble down towards the train station, and see what presents itself?" G. suggested when I bemoaned the lack of Kentish palm trees. Agreeing somewhat mournfully to this (it would've been rather fun living in a palm tree hut in central Canterbury!) we hefted our backpacks and began to walk.

Chapter 41

Salvation. The journey home. Our
pilgrimage begins.

It was a sorry trio (plus Monty the dog) that traipsed defeated away from Canterbury Cathedral, for so many days the hope and goal of our hearts. We weren't even sure if we'd completed our pilgrimage. The whole point, as I saw it anyway, was as an atonement for past misdeeds, and as a prologue to a new and better sort of life. Or something of that ilk anyway. I know I had some vague and half-conceived notions of the absolute rightness and fitness of our undertaking, but had I been asked the exact details of what I was doing, or what I expected the result to be, I would have been seven different kinds of stumped. I hadn't expected a ray of light from the clouds, and a booming voice proclaiming 'These are my beloved sons, with whom I am well pleased (and Monty the dog)'. I had not expected scales from the eyes (yuck!) or for my chains to fall off, or anything, well, anything *flashy*. Nothing too impressive and tasteless you know. I do know that I had expected something; anything but this dissatisfaction and feeling of immense anti-climax.

And then, of course, it started raining again. I cannot remember a time in my life when I have felt so defeated, so thoroughly demoralised. My companions clearly felt equally disappointed, and we marched with shoulders slumped and heads bowed. I don't know about Monty. I spared him not a glance, but had no doubt that he was revelling in our despair.

"Excuse me?" A deep, warm voice brought me out of my morose reverie. I looked up and blinked at the chap who stood before me. He wore a ragged jacket and jeans, and had dark brown hair and stubbly beard, and I was struck by a strong feeling of familiarity.

I peered at him, and then drew in a breath. "You're the tramp! The one selling the Big Issue!"

"I think it's generally considered more polite to say 'homeless person' than tramp, but yes, that was me."

"Look, I'm really terribly sorry, and I was going to buy a copy when we came back that way, but things have gone a little bit wrong you see and..."

"That's quite alright. Don't worry about it."

G. was staring hard at this odd but pleasant-seeming fellow. "I say, aren't you the chap from the boating pond? The one with the rope for people who fall in?"

"I don't know about that. My father has a boating pond, and he does like to make sure that not too many people drown in it, it's true. I am told that the family resemblance is extremely strong."

B. was peering at him as well. "Really? I could've sworn I saw you in the river, teaching that lad not to drown."

The man smiled, as though slightly embarrassed. "That could have been me, yes. It certainly isn't unknown."

"Have you been following us?" I asked suspiciously. This fellow was starting to sound like a proper weirdo and no mistake!

"Follow you?" He seemed slightly amused. "On the

contrary, wherever you've been, I was there already."

This didn't really sound any better. In fact it sounded darned sinister if you ask me. "You mean you were waiting for us?"

"In a matter of speaking, I suppose so, yes."

"Well I call it very dodgy! Ambushing us all over the place when we aren't expecting it, and watching us all the time. I find it all very peculiar. There are police registers for people like you."

He smiled again, amused. "I've been everywhere you've been going. I've been waiting for you there because I knew which way you were going to go, but that you came at all, and the way you travelled when you did were entirely up to you."

"Well a fat lot of good it did us! We've not been able to afford to get into the cathedral and finish our pilgrimage, and now we can't even get home again."

A slight frown clouded the man's brow for a moment, but he smiled again. "That's exactly what I wanted to talk to you about. I'll happily give you the money to get home."

I blinked in surprise. "Um, I'm very grateful and all, but if you're on the streets of Canterbury selling the Big Issue, when you're not not-drowning children or boating on your dad's pond, then I can hardly see that you can afford to pay for three of us to get all the way home."

"Ah, well I can afford it you see, so that's not a problem. My father's actually quite rich."

My eyes narrowed. "Very rich? Almost a millionaire, one might say?"

"I suppose so, yes. I really don't know how rich he is."

"So you'll be able to sleep in a nice warm bed tonight regardless?" G. asked.

"No, no. I'm afraid my father's sort of, well 'cast out'

isn't the right word at all. 'Sent into the world' is perhaps better, but only for a little while. I'll be going back soon."

"Well then you need the money for a hostel or a B&B or something."

"I absolutely insist that you take it." He dug his hand into a pocket and thrust a wodge of notes at me, which I took.

"I'm really not sure we can accept..." But he was already turning away and walking off.

"It's okay," he called over his shoulder. "Only another three days until I get to go home."

"But I didn't even buy a Big Issue..." I trailed off as he disappeared round a corner.

I looked at the money he'd given us, and calculated that it would cover our three train fares, and still give us enough money for a cup of tea each at the station.

I was frankly baffled at the fellow's behaviour. By my reckoning, this was about one hundred Big Issue's worth of money he'd just handed over. It seemed an act of the rankest stupidity and foolishness to give up everything he had at present to help three wayward souls such as ourselves, and I said as much.

G. shrugged. "It seems that amazingly foolish generosity runs in the family. I'm sure he'll be alright."

B. tutted. "We should have asked him if his father could include us in that backwards lottery of his. We missed a trick there."

As we talked, we headed through Canterbury in the direction of the train station. We reached it and passed through, purchasing tickets with the rather rumpled cash that the lunatic fellow had given us. Handing over the money was, frankly, a bit of a wrench. I couldn't help but feel that I had come by it dishonestly, and that by using it, I was guilty of something little short of theft. Why would that chap have given us the money, when he could have kept it for himself and lived in comfort until he could go home?

We boarded our train, and as we trundled out of the station, I stared out of the window, and the rain running in rivulets down the glass and heaved a sigh.

"Well that's it then," I said heavily. "We've completed our pilgrimage."

"Yes, we have," G. agreed.

"A job well done," B. added with a satisfied nod. "We've walked ourselves ragged, and reached the cathedral, and now we can go home and put any silly notions of sin out of our heads and get on with enjoying our lives. After all, we're Good People now."

"I'm not entirely sure that that's how it works," I said, still staring out across the rain-sodden landscape. "We haven't really done anything, and the most important bit seems to have been done by someone else."

G. nodded. "I suspect that it's rather more complicated than you might like to think B. The important things in life usually are."

I sighed mournfully. "In fact, I think that what we've just done was the easy bit."

B. looked aghast. "The easy bit? Easy? My feet are rubbed raw and my legs are on the verge of dropping off! I refuse to believe that that was the easy bit!"

"It seems to me that the whole thing was just us getting our boots on," I said. "We may have stubbed our toe on the boot-scraper more than once, and I've no doubt that we've got an awful lot of mud on the carpet, but we're finally ready."

"Ready for what though," G. mused. "I'm still

unconvinced. I mean, it seems as though there might very well be something more, but if there is, I'm not sure what. I think I'm going to take a long view of the whole thing, and wait and see."

"Piffle!" B. snorted. "I think the whole thing's been a tremendous waste of time. Oh, not that I haven't enjoyed it J.," he added quickly. "Very good for us I shouldn't imagine, and we've met some very, um, interesting people, but I think I'll go home and get on with things, and try not to read any more upsetting pamphlets. Or let you read them either!"

I remained silent, and the three of us, and even Monty who was curled up on G.'s boot, were quiet for the rest of the trip. Considering the time and effort that had been involved in getting to Canterbury, the ease with which we returned was almost obscene. In only a few hours, we were passing through familiar countryside and into the comforting sight of home. The unappreciated miracles of the modern age and so on.

We disembarked and passed through the station, where we prepared to part and go our separate ways, back to warm homes and comfortable, familiar things. I turned to my companions.

"No, having thought on it long and hard, I think I've decided that we didn't complete our pilgrimage after all. I apologise for that, not that it was really my fault of course. But then, I'm not sure that we would have completed it even if we had got in. I think that we've got our boots on, and now we're standing on the doorstep, with our hats in our hands, and our bags on our backs. Now all it needs is a small act of will to set us going along the road. I think that I'd very much like the two of you to come with me, but I understand if you don't want to. I suspect that it will be very hard, and not very comfortable, and I suspect that it will take a very long time, but that ultimately, it will be well worth it. Both the journey itself and the destination. I've learnt an awful lot about walking the road these last few days, and I want to put it into practice. So there you are. I think for now though, it's time for bed."

I turned and started to walk away, but stopped, wrestling with my conscience. Such a mental and moral duel I have never fought, but eventually my better nature triumphed, sweaty and bloodied, and I capitulated with considerable bad grace. I turned back to them. "Oh, and G.? I... suppose you can bring Monty too." Thus exhausted, I prepared to go home.

"J.," G. called after me. I turned to him. "It's not that late yet. Let's all go home and drop off our things and pick up a bit of cash, and I'll see you in the pub in forty minutes."

I smiled. "G. old chap, I think that sounds absolutely perfect."

THE END

Acknowledgements

This book has taken a very long time to write, and many of the ideas and analogies that I've used have occurred to me during conversations with other people, often with very different beliefs and opinions to myself. In trying to explain my position, I may not have persuaded them, but I have learnt an awful lot about what I do and don't believe, and why.

Firstly and most importantly, I'd like to thank my wife Caroline, both for her love and support, for insisting on asking difficult questions when I want to go to sleep, for spurring me on to actually try and get this published, and for helping get the wording right.

I would very much like to thank all those people who met in the Cwmanne Tavern on Thursday nights, both those who participated in the frequent, repeated and lengthy theological and philosophical debates, and those who merely tolerated them and were just there for the folk music and to play cards.

I'd also like to thank Whispering Tree for their invaluable advice, help and hard work in publishing and publicising this book.

About the Author

Thomas Jones, the son of a Methodist minister, was born in Stoke-on-Trent, and grew up in many different places all over England. Perhaps as a result of the frequent changes in location, he started making up stories from a very young age, and creative writing was his favourite subject throughout school. Early stories were mostly fantasies that were completely ruined by an unimaginative teacher. This did not stop him, and at university he continued to write fiction as a way of avoiding writing essays. His interest in writing led him to take a course in creative writing, at which point it became the work he was trying to avoid. Once that was out of his system, he took it up again for the pure enjoyment of it. He tends to write the kind of things that he would love to read if it weren't him writing them.

Thomas studied both archaeology and creative writing at the University of Wales Lampeter.